Written, Illustrated & Designed in Ukraine
Printed in the United Kingdom

The Black Sea WHALE

A Beacon in the Sea of Troubles

Editor-in-Chief: Ulana Suprun
Managing Editor: Viktoriia Antonenko

Copy Editors: James Merritt and Kate Kelley
Production Supervisor: Irina Yurchenko
Associate Editor: Nazar Tokar
Stories written by Marichka Melnyk, Viktoriia Antonenko, Mary Mycio, Sergej Sumlenny, Oleksii Dubrov, Janusz Bugajski and **illustrated by** Ivan Voliansky, Kateryna Sova, Iryna Lysenko, Maryna Lutsyk, Oleh Smal, Andrii Yermolenko, Olenka Zahorodnyk, Mykhailo Aleksandrov, Oleksandr Terez.
Titans of translation include Ardis Chrystal, Stefko Bandera, Marta Olynyk.
Cover illustrated by Julia Maystruk.
Journal designed by Zakhar Kryvoshyya and Oksana Vaskiv.
Additional design by Oleksandr Maystruk.
The font **Kamenyar** is designed by Zakhar Kryvoshyya and **Humus** is designed by Andrij Shevchenko.
Produced by Marko Suprun.

WWW.BLACKSEAWHALE.COM
The Black Sea Whale is published by Rogue Umbrella, LTD.
ISBN 978-1-7385616-0-5

Please send reprint, corrections, or other inquiries to: story@blackseawhale.com
If you are interested in writing or illustrating for *The Black Sea Whale*, please send an email to: story@blackseawhale.com
Printed by Park Communications, a Carbon Neutral Company, on FSC® certified paper.

Published by Rogue Umbrella, LTD.
Lynton House, 7-12 Tavistock Square
London, WC1H 9LT, United Kingdom

Through the long, dark night inscrutable
Never will I close my wearied eyes,
Searching ever for that guiding star—
Radiant empress of the midnight skies.

Yes, through all my tears I still will smile,
Sing my songs though troubles round me loom;
Hopeless, still hope on against all odds,
I will live! Away, ye thoughts of gloom!

—LESYA UKRAINKA
Excerpt from "Contra Spem Spero"
Translated by Percival Cundy

CONTENTS

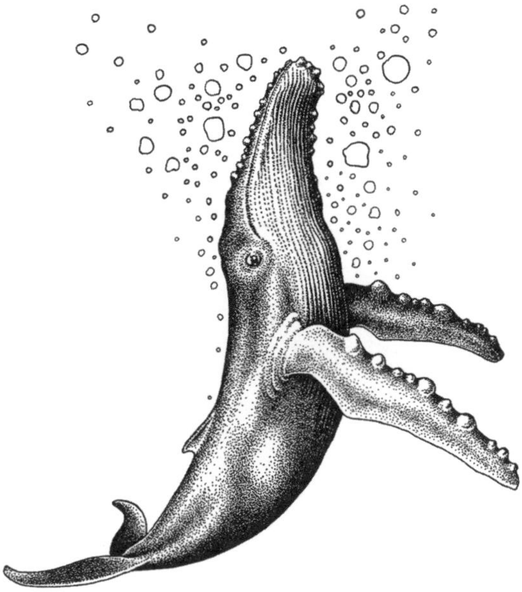

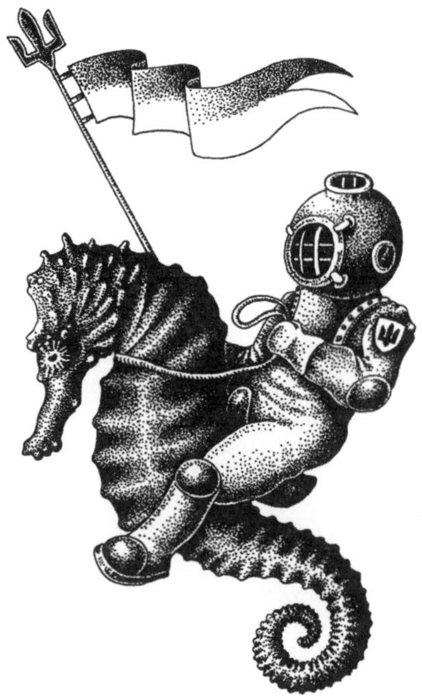

THE BLACK SEA WHALE SONG

JUST BEFORE A STRETCHED MEMORY snaps with the past like a rubber band, at the same place where an echo becomes a whisper, beneath the ringing cacophony of Achaen and Trojan swords clashing in the tumultuous war over Helen of Troy along the Aegean coast of Asia Minor, an island arose from the waters of the Black Sea — a sea the ancient Greeks regarded as "inhospitable." The island was called *Lewke*, the Greek word for white. Today this island is known as *Zmiinyi* or Snake Island.

According to legend, the island was created by the sea nymph Thetis. After 17 days of mourning for her son Achilles, who had died in battle at the gates of Troy after Paris targeted an arrow at the only vulnerable spot on his body — his heel, the grief-stricken Thetis raised a snow-white rocky island from the depths of the sea. It was to become the last refuge for her only and beloved child.

Later, a stone temple in honour of Achilles was built on the island. Greek ships would invariably pay homage to memories there when traversing the waters from the metropolis to their colonies on the Northern Black Sea coast or vice versa, when returning home. Over time, the ancient Greeks became more familiar with these lands, now the sovereign territory of Ukraine. Having explored the shores, inlets, and harbours, their unease transformed into admiration, and they now saw the Black Sea as "hospitable," designating it as peaceful and safe for many years to come (albeit, with a few exceptions).

At the beginning of Russia's invasion of Ukraine, Snake Island quickly became a symbol of national resistance. The commander of a Russian battleship threatened 13 Ukrainian border guards stationed there with death and destruction if they did not surrender. They flatly refused, with a reply that would rally a nation: "Russian warship, go fuck yourself!" Those guardians of Snake Island became talismans of Ukrainian tenacity, proving to everyone, no trouble is so great as to coerce the loss of belief in yourself.

Today, pundits, politicians, and other purveyors of doom have worn out the meaning of an "existential crisis," making surviving one, unfairly pedestrian. Bereft of solutions to life's questions, and having themselves launched salvos of troubles, from inflation to healthcare, all products of failed leadership, egos become deliberately inflated casting dark shadows on common sense solutions to treatable symptoms of a complicated life. It is no surprise that in this ecology, suicide emerges as an option, especially when popular culture sanitises the pressure to surrender rather than champion resistance.

Whether or not to take up arms against yourself, to capitulate to life's challenges, is not a new question, having been pondered, poetically, by William Shakespeare, in *Hamlet*, Act III, Scene I:

To be, or not to be: that is the question:
Whether 'tis nobler in the mind to suffer
The slings and arrows of outrageous fortune,
Or to take arms against a sea of troubles,
And by opposing end them? To die: to sleep...

But how does a country, a people, or a nation answer his question when faced with another genocide? Turns out, questions posed by poets are often answered by soldiers: the Guardians of Snake Island in the Black Sea have become beacons, showing us how to sail through a sea of troubles.

The same coast where Greek, and later Roman, Byzantine, Genoese, Ottoman, and many other ships have long been docked, is regularly shelled by Russia's military. The Russian Federation's Ministry of Defence threatens to attack any foreign ships entering its waters. Anti-ship mines are surfing its waves instead of Ukrainian and foreign vacationers.

Ukraine, however, is not surrendering: archaeologists of the future exploring the bottom of the Black Sea will discover several artefacts from the turbulent Ukrainian present, at least one of which will be a Russian missile cruiser, the Kremlin's flagship *Moskva*, resting on the seabed near Snake Island since 14 April 2022.

Ukrainians surprised the Western world by resisting the first days of Russia's full-scale invasion, despite the fact everyone was betting on a lightning-speed victory for Russia, considered the second greatest army in the world (although most sympathised with the underdog). Experts (many without expertise) in capitals such as Berlin, London, and Washington, DC, even hoped for a quick decapitation of Kyiv's leadership. Ukraine continues to astonish the West because Ukrainians will not supplicate to Putin. Kyiv's leadership has embraced a principled position to not trade sovereign lands or individual agency in exchange for an ersatz peace from a street thug, a dictator who dreams of reviving the Russian Empire.

Ukrainians, like the Black Sea whale, did not exist for the international community. Hidden under the dark and stormy layers of propaganda and disinformation, often disguised as literature, Ukrainians have spent more than a century holding their breath, ascending from the depths of the sea to the surface, to finally exhale and assert their true name. Ukraine's national consolidation is its strongest weapon, and it will break the bonds of the Russian Empire's cultural appropriation which branded Ukrainians as "Little Russians" or "Soviets," a prison moniker forced on Ukrainians by the Soviet Union.

Western journalists were amazed to see Ukrainians as distinct, even cool. In an interview with the BBC in March 2023, Foreign Minister Dmytro Kuleba replied, "Historically, Ukraine was unfavourably underappreciated. And I regret it took bloodshed and a devastating war for the world to realise how cool we are. And we were always cool. But it just took you too much time to realise that." Indeed, we were cool, before 24 February 2022, or February–March 2014, or 24 August 1991. But Western perceptions of Ukraine were framed by Moscow – the centre of a LARP empire – whose leaders excelled at cosplaying a powerful political force, when in reality, it was simply a Potemkin village.

It's OK to admit you have been living under a misapprehension. There's been a lot of flotsam polluting the waters of a good faith conversation between Kyiv and its western partners in London, Brussels, Washington, and other capitals.

Military cooperation between Kyiv, London, Brussels, and Washington shouldn't be a fountain of anxiety (except maybe in Moscow, and that's not a bad thing). Weapons in Ukrainian hands are not for suicide, but for self-defence; not in order to avoid the "sea of troubles," but to prepare and plan for the challenges posed by an aggressive neighbour; to stop them here, between two worlds, on the barricade between two civilisations: one where the rule of law reigns, and the other where abject violence and brute force set the agenda.

To help clear and navigate the waters, we decided to launch *The Black Sea Whale.*

The Black Sea Whale is a new publication, with lyrics from a long-forgotten whale song emanating from the raging waters of the hospitable sea ebbing and flowing over the temporarily Russian-occupied Ukrainian Crimean Peninsula and Ukraine's sovereign Snake Island. Carried on the current for thousands of kilometres, this song can be heard around the world connecting the past, present, and future of Ukraine and its people with Western civilisation, which we have been a part of since ancient times.

The stories in *The Black Sea Whale* (a "thirdly" publication, as opposed to a quarterly) are a second chance for the world: not just to listen, but to hear the sincere and true voice of Ukrainians, and to discover authentic Ukraine and its polyphony. They are about the prosaic and the extraordinary, about who we were, who we are, and who we can be. Some stories resemble reality so vividly, they are hard to believe, while others are so outlandish, they strike you as being true. Sometimes they are ironically comedic, at other times heart-wrenchingly sad, but always self-critical and reflect the lessons we have learnt throughout life. You might find echoes of your own life in the specifics of Ukraine, in this bespoke publication for the English-speaking world, because the challenges we face are universal be they in Kyiv or London or where you might be reading this.

These are stories we would want to read ourselves.

In her story in the inaugural issue of *The Black Sea Whale,* Marichka Melnyk comes to the conclusion: "Good enemies don't exist, and neither do innocent traitors," after living under Russian occupation in her village outside Kyiv for 34 days. Witnessing the behaviour of her fellow villagers and their attitudes toward the Russian occupiers, she poses a difficult question: Is there a place for traitors in post-victory Ukraine? In her answer, she draws parallels with the policy toward collaborators in the post-WWII de-occupied Netherlands.

"I work as much as I'm paid," "It's not in my job description," "I won't get a bonus anyway," "Can't anyone else do it?" Consider yourself lucky if these verbal parasites haven't poisoned your daily professional life. When most of the ship's crew is beset with demotivation, relying on a successful voyage is foolish and fraught with consequence. Viktoriia Antonenko introduces you to the world of Soviet values, preserved like museum relics scattered throughout all spheres of life.

As soon as Russian troops occupied Chornobyl in February 2022, an ominous cloud of fear drifted over Ukraine once again. After the nuclear power plant accident in 1986, Ukrainians routinely blamed Chornobyl for all their troubles. Although Russia's occupation of Ukraine's Donbas replaced it as the focus of all of Ukraine's ills in 2014, the

Chornobyl Zone of Alienation continues to cause dread. Mary Mycio (1959–2022) reveals the heroes, real and imaginary, thanks to whom alienation is eventually replaced by rebirth. And she is not afraid to expose the real culprit behind both catastrophes.

Ukraine is not the only country stuck in a toxic relationship with Russia. The almost maniacal fascination with the "great" Russian culture and "mystical" Russian nature, including an unhealthy obsession with Russia as a vital partner at the expense of other global relationships, is a national characteristic of Germans, regardless of political party preference. Sergej Sumlenny reveals the origins of Berlin's deep-seated infatuation with Moscow and how it has been affected by Russia's full-scale invasion of Ukraine.

The desperate act of self-immolation in Kaunas by the hippie Romas Kalanta in the spring of 1972 became a litmus test for Lithuanians who still remembered living in an independent state and perceived the Soviets as occupiers. The collective memory of the Baltic nations turned out to be stronger than that of Ukrainians. Oleksii Dubrov shows us how Lithuania weaves the threads of history into a portrait of their rebirth even if the yarn may be frayed.

Cartographers have been mapping the environment to bring about a better understanding of the world we live in for centuries. Janusz Bugajski, senior fellow at *The Jamestown Foundation*, analyses the fragile foundations of the Russian Federation and uncovers new opportunities waiting for the colonised, non-Russian captive nations following the inevitable transformation of Russia from Empire to State.

"I woke up that day to the sound of explosions and the whistling of missiles as they flew by my window and crashed into the centre of Moscow." Is there safety in any of the five zones of occupation into which the city of Moscow is divided in 2049? Oleksii Dubrov's story gives us a glimpse into the future, where a Ukrainian orphan discovers a secret as Russians struggle with imperial debris between the Ural Mountains and the Far East.

Thank you for sharing an interest in Ukrainians and their creative contributions in this, the inaugural issue of *The Black Sea Whale*.

Enjoy the song and keep reading.

The Editors
The Black Sea Whale

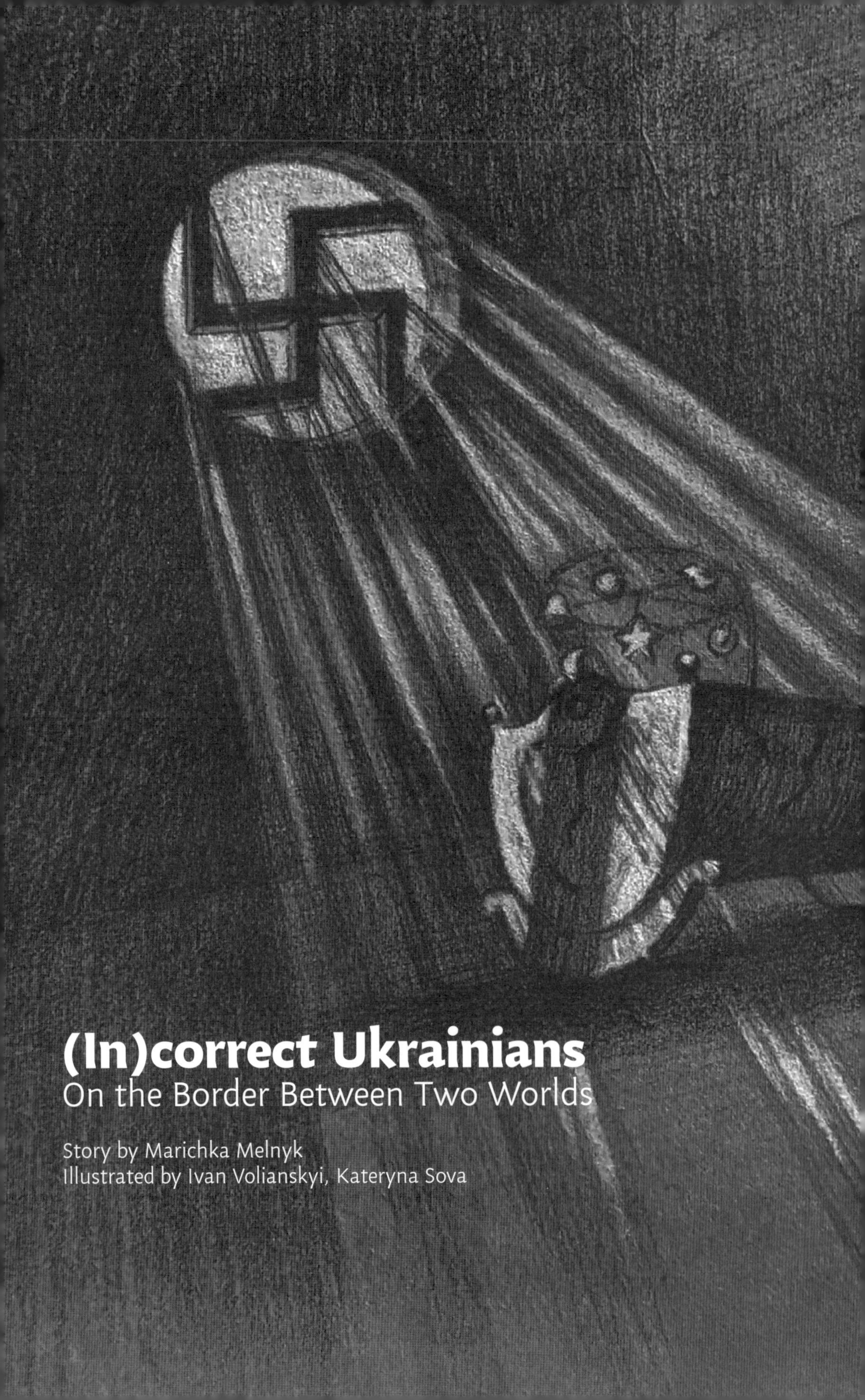

(In)correct Ukrainians

On the Border Between Two Worlds

Story by Marichka Melnyk
Illustrated by Ivan Volianskyi, Kateryna Sova

THE FIRST RUSSIAN SOLDIERS invaded my village north of Kyiv at dawn on 25 February 2022. I was awakened at around 5.00am by a crescendo of rumbling engines and the clatter of rattling windows. The fold-out sofa bed I was lying on began vibrating. Soon, it felt as if the whole house was shaking. Surreptitiously peering out the front window from behind the curtains, I watched as a slow-moving but constant, seemingly endless, convoy passed by our house, made up of armoured personnel carriers, tanks, self-propelled artillery, Grad rocket launchers, fuel trucks, tractor trailers, amphibious rigs, vehicles carrying radio jamming equipment – and a sea of trucks carrying soldiers. All the vehicles were emblazoned with the letter "V" in white paint.

I was paralysed by the sight. My brain was unable to piece together a sentence and my fingers stumbled over the letters on the keyboard of my phone. I sent a message about the movement of enemy vehicles through our village to the Facebook page of the ground forces of Ukraine's army. I must have typed those sorry 14 words at a rate of about one word per minute, and then I spent half an hour waiting for a reply (don't ask me why I thought someone would actually reply).

One could only guess what path the Russian soldiers had taken on their way to our village, but their next destination was obvious. My parents' house, from which, barely breathing, I watched this terrifying scene, is on route P02, the road which leads directly to Kyiv. On any normal day, it takes just under an hour to reach the capital.

The procession of Russian vehicles went on for two and a half hours. They didn't hang around for long, but left behind the first (and, unfortunately, not the last) bullet-ridden car – a white 1998 Opel Corsa that had carelessly driven towards them. The man behind the wheel and the woman in the front seat were killed. They were shot 200m from my home. After 30 seconds of machine-gun fire, followed by the deafening grind of crushing metal and the sound of shattering glass, the Russian invasion force moved on.

The subsequent convoys driving through the village had fewer vehicles. At first, they just passed through, but after a while, they started stopping: sometimes to wait for those lagging behind, other times to set up a field kitchen. But mainly they stopped alongside people's houses to take cover from the shelling by the Ukrainian military, which had formed a buffer zone to stop the enemy from entering the capital.

We couldn't see all of this, but we heard it.

By we, I mean my mum, my dad, and myself. And also my brother, Andriy, and his wife, my sister and her husband, Oleh, and my two nieces and one nephew. They came to the village immediately after Russia fired missiles at our military airports and depots on 24 February, thinking it would be safer to ride out the war here rather than in Kyiv.

"Riding out the war," we quickly became sensitive to the faintest vibrations and could predict the approach of enemy convoys before they appeared on the horizon. When the Russian military was in the village, we spent our time lying on the floor of our veranda (the room in my parents' house furthest from the street) or hiding in the cellar. On the first day the Russians came into the village, we carried two wooden pallets, old mattresses, pillows, blankets, candles, matches, a 19-litre sized bottle of drinking water (the kind you'd find in an office on top of a water cooler), and a small shovel down to the cellar.

We chose our hiding spot depending on the proximity and intensity of shooting.

Every minute spent in expectation of danger seemed like an eternity, with no beginning or end. Every onset of darkness dredged up all our inner fears, with visions of the countless unpleasant scenarios awaiting us if Ukraine fell. Every sunrise brought the hope all of this was just a nightmare, and we would wake up to no war. But our hopes were futile.

The electricity and phone service in our village were cut off on the morning of the third day of the Russian invasion, and along with them the opportunity to help our defenders by giving them information about the enemy's movements. The only remaining option was to "help" the Russians find their way around. Armed with a crowbar, my brother Andriy and brother-in-law Oleh went to remove road signs. Their first expedition went off without a hitch, but the next one...

In the late afternoon of 28 February 2022, another horde, barrelling down both lanes of the two-lane highway, turned off the main road and took up positions in our village. Soldiers with guns broke into almost every second house, brazenly telling the owners, "We're moving in!" They parked their vehicles in the local park and turned the school and community centre into a command post and military hospital. By nightfall, there were checkpoints on all the streets, regardless of whether they were main roads or small lanes. Machine gun fire rang out from time to time.

We were under occupation.

Andriy and Oleh started heading back from their "secret mission" around dusk.

They were no more than 150m away from home when an armoured personnel carrier and a military jeep stopped on Bila Street, which they needed to cross to get home. Half a dozen soldiers poured out of the vehicles to greet them.

There was no doubt to whom these soldiers had sworn allegiance. Wearing uniforms covered in as many orange and black ribbons as fleas found on an unwashed dog, the language they spoke gave them away – the tone, rhythm, tempo, and accent weren't the same as "our" Russian.

My brother and brother-in-law dropped the crowbar and tried to hide behind a nearby fence, albeit unsuccessfully. They were caught and searched, forced to strip to the waist. The soldiers checked them for "Nazi" tattoos and marks or bruises on their skin from the kickback of a gun or a bulletproof vest and looked for traces of gunpowder on their hands. They held them at gunpoint while they looked through the call logs, messages, and photos on their phones. Having found nothing incriminating, they let Andriy and Oleh go.

Before letting them go, though, one of the occupiers, an ethnic Buryat, said arrogantly, "We're here to bring order," savouring each word. "Go and tell everyone!"

"Never. Never again in my life will I utter a single word in Russian. And I won't respond to it either," my brother summed up when he got home and recounted his experience.

Andriy is the oldest of the three of us. He's three years older than my sister and nine years older than me. He was the first to leave our village to study at one of the universities in Kyiv. I rarely think about the age difference, but it did have a major impact on certain things. Kyiv in 1998, when my brother moved there, and Kyiv in 2007, when I followed suit, were two very different cities linguistically. He had zero chance of not speaking Russian.

The whole family gathered on the veranda where, since the invasion, we began spending our evenings together.

The door was locked, the windows tightly covered with sheets, and a candle on the table flickered, casting shifting shadows on the walls. The rest of the house was completely dark. Everyone was fully dressed, to be ready to run to the cellar, and had their emergency “go bag” by their side.

Andriy sat on the chair next to me and I could feel his whole body shaking.

His fear was contagious, infecting everyone in the room. We all knew his encounter with the Russian “order-restorers” could have ended very differently. There was a deep silence. My imagination was filled with gory images that turned my stomach. I felt like I was sitting on a bed of nails.

“All my colleagues speak Ukrainian,” I said to break the oppressive silence, taking a sip of tea from a coffee cup decorated with a Mochy Mantoo sticker.

“Most of the people where I work are Russian speakers, but they switch to Ukrainian with me,” my sister observed from the ottoman where she sat rocking her three-year-old daughter. “Although the change happened only recently, after the Maidan.”

“Hardly anyone in my office speaks Ukrainian, maybe two or three people,” my brother chimed in. “But from now on, they can go to hell with their Russian!”

“After all, if war isn’t reason enough to stop speaking Russian, then I don’t know what is,” I added. I was truly happy with Andriy’s decision, but I knew it was wrong to attribute it to the war. The war was in its ninth year, and he chose to speak his native language only when coming face to face with it.

Despite my attempts at conversation, silence again filled the room. But at least now the silence sounded Ukrainian.

“IS YOUR WATER OK?” OUR NEIGHbour asked my mother as she peered over the garden fence the following morning. A stranger was standing next to our neighbour. My brother and I stood off to the side, listening to the conversation from our porch.

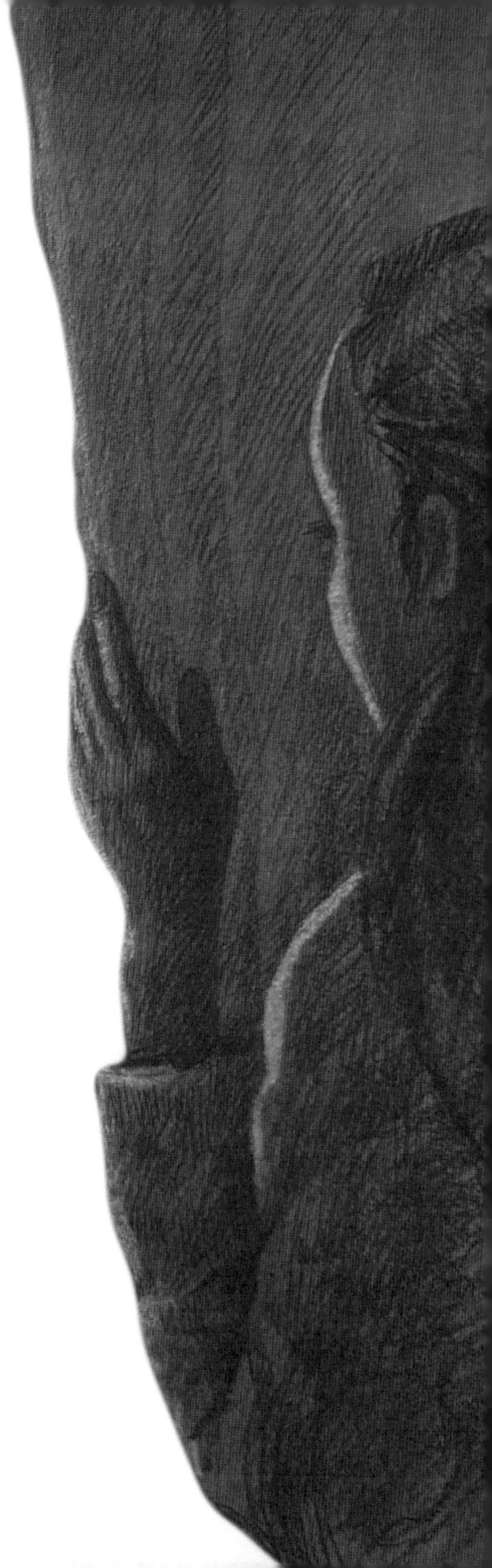

The neighbour's name is Lesia. She lives one house over from us and is relatively new to our street, so I don't know much about her. Lesia is from the Poltava region, under 40, twice married, twice divorced, and has two children. Those are the only facts I know about her – the rest are rumours. Supposedly, her first husband is in the militia of the ORDLO (the temporarily occupied territories of Donetsk and Luhansk Oblasts). The second husband, with whom she's still living, is also a real winner. As soon as the first shots rang out, he took his biological son, the younger of Lesia's children, and went to stay at his parents' house deeper in the village, leaving Lesia behind with the older son.

"Are you kidding? You need electricity to pump water from the drilled well and the water from our dug well is rusty. I can't remember the last time we cleaned it... You don't have anywhere to get water?" my mother asked, concerned.

"I do! I'm staying at Serhiy's place," Lesia nodded at the man standing next to her, who turned out to be the neighbour on the other side of our garden. "He took me and Vitaliy in because everything we have is electric. It's so cold in our house our teeth won't stop chattering. He at least has a wood-burning stove..."

"What were you celebrating all night, almost till dawn?" my mother asked. "The whole house was lit up and it was really noisy and disturbing."

"Well, the Russians came to the house last night. First, they checked every nook and cranny in the place, then decided to take hot baths. We started up the generator in the yard and it was running half the night heating water so they could wash off the dirt from the road. They drank tea to warm up because they were freezing cold, but the water we have is no good for tea..."

"So, you're asking for water for whom exactly? The Russians?" my mother asked, puzzled.

"They're OK guys!" Lesia stubbornly tried to convince my mother, while Serhiy vigorously nodded in agreement as if to add credence to Lesia's words. "They didn't know where they were going. Their commanders gave them rations for two days and told them they were being sent for training..." our neighbour was quoting Russian propaganda verbatim, oblivious to what she was doing.

"OK guys?! What about the people they shot and killed, just like that, for no reason?!" Andriy burst out next to me. He turned around and stormed off before Lesia could respond. I stood there, lost in thought.

SERHIY'S HOUSE IS ON THE STREET where the Russian soldiers crossed paths with my brother and brother-in-law. To the best of my recollection, it was once called *Sovietska* (Soviet Street). They decided to rename it in 2015, before I moved back in with my parents. At first, I was happy to hear decommunization was finally taking place in my village, like it was in the rest of Ukraine. But my excitement faded when I heard the new name: *Bila* (White). Seriously? If the goal was to pick the most meaningless and empty name possible, then my fellow villagers earned an A+ on the assignment. The only thing this renaming showed was their inability to reflect on the history of Ukraine in the 20th century and make a clear statement regarding the Soviet past.

And now we're dealing with those direct consequences. Modern-day Soviets – the direct descendants of those who 100 years ago couldn't accept the declaration of independence by the Ukrainian People's Republic and forced the USSR on us – have literally come knocking on our doors, again armed with machine guns, declaring "there is no such country as Ukraine."

"OUR GUYS LEFT," LESIA SAID IN Russian, sighing forlornly, holding two Thermoses of cold water above the wooden fence separating us.

Our village had been without electricity for three weeks now. My family was lucky, since our house is hooked up to natural gas.

But many people in our village, who relied on electricity for heating and cooking, had to improvise. For example, our neighbours on the right had to move their kitchen to the garden behind their house: the owner made a makeshift stovetop-oven out of bricks. They had taken Lesia in with her older son after Serhiy's home had been seized and inhabited by the Russians.

To stretch their rations of firewood, our neighbours lit the homemade stove only once a day, usually around lunchtime. They tried to make do with the one meal at lunchtime, only drinking tea in the morning and evening. My mother invited our neighbours to use our gas stove, but they declined. From time to time, they would ask us to heat some water for them, but no more than that.

"Why did Lesia suddenly start speaking Russian? And what guys left?" These thoughts flashed in my head as I headed toward the fence, carefully hopping between the white snowdrops and yellow and purple crocuses to avoid crushing the plants in my mother's flowerbed. As I stepped with one foot onto a tree stump to reach for the water containers, I looked over the fence where my neighbour stood with an unhappy look on her face. *"She really is sad. It's not my imagination,"* I thought.

Sad, but as they say in our village, in full "combat" splendour with black pencilled-in eyebrows, eyeliner, mascara, foundation, blush, lipstick (or was it lip gloss?), her blond hair in a high ponytail, a manicure, new tracksuit, and lots and lots of lavender perfume.

Lesia's appearance was in stark contrast to mine.

I hadn't washed my hair in a week. It was so greasy you could fry an egg on it. When you have 10 people living in a house instead of the usual three, every drop of shampoo is as valuable as gold. Forget about makeup — my face hadn't even seen moisturiser for 18 days. My nails were cut down to the nub, but dirt still somehow found its way underneath them.

I was wearing my brother's pants, which my mum had altered for me at some point, although they were still too long and I had to roll them up, and a stretched-out hand-woven sweater I had worn years ago as a university student. I wanted to be warm and comfortable and not have to care about keeping my clothes clean when I went to the barn to help my parents with the goats (and I stank to prove it). Lesia, on the other hand, looked like she was getting ready for a date, or had just come back from one.

"Good morning!" I called out a greeting, as I grabbed the thermoses from Lesia... and immediately bit my tongue.

Over the past few weeks, this normal greeting had become completely inappropriate. It flew out of your mouth automatically and left behind a bitter aftertaste, like you get after eating a grapefruit. It sounded like a gibe — what goddamn kind of "good" morning could there be when you hadn't slept all night because you were counting artillery fire or enemy helicopters circling overhead instead of sheep? People immediately followed with an apologetic "Well, if you can say that," and dropped their gaze to the ground, as if racked in guilt. Once, a neighbour said, "It's a new day!" instead of the usual greeting as he approached me with his one-and-a-half-year-old son. These words, in my opinion, better reflected our new reality, the one where you didn't know if you'd live to see tomorrow.

"Who left?" I asked Lesia as I leant against the wooden fence pole trying not to fall while balancing on one leg.

"Our guys..." I still had no clue who she was talking about because there weren't any Ukrainian soldiers in our village. There were rumours about a detachment, which was supposed to have deployed to our village, but our guys weren't able to take up positions before the Russian soldiers came, and then it became impossible. She saw my raised eyebrows and explained: "The guys who were stationed here," and pointed to the opposite end of the gardens, to ~~Sovietska~~ Bila Street.

Her answer literally knocked me off my feet. I lost my balance and fell off the stump, trampling my mother's flowers. *"Am I hearing things?"* I thought. I couldn't believe my ears.

I didn't get back up onto the stump to continue the conversation; instead, I quietly turned around and took the Thermoses to our house to boil water for tea.

The wooden fence no longer provided a sense of protection nor seemed like a reliable barrier.

"THERE'S SOMETHING I DON'T get about Lesia's behaviour," I opened the discussion at dinner when my family gathered on the veranda that evening. The conversation with our neighbour that morning was still bothering me.

"What don't you understand?" asked my mother, as she stood by the open kitchen door preparing swill for the baby goats.

"For one thing, she calls the occupiers 'our guys.' She makes them tea so the poor fellas don't get too cold. She dresses up for them like she's going out on a date. She speaks Russian, which she never used to," I sat on the ottoman next to the table, listing everything confusing me.

"Well, she's a young, single woman. Maybe she's looking for a husband. Her next one," my sister-in-law suggested, shrugging her shoulders.

"Maybe, but... What if our neighbour is a collaborator?" I said, having found the courage to voice my suspicion.

"What does that word mean?" my mother asked.

"It comes from the English 'to collaborate' – to cooperate. A collaborator is someone – he or SHE," I emphasised, "who cooperates with the enemy of their country during war. The word isn't as widely used here because in the Soviet Union they were more often called 'traitors of the Homeland' or 'accomplices of the fascists'."

"Aren't you being a bit extreme? What does Lesia have to do with that?" my mother tried to defend our neighbour.

"Mum, you can collaborate in different ways. You don't necessarily have to dig trenches with the Russians or hand them artillery shells." I was standing my ground. "In the USSR, you could wind up on the list of 'traitors of the Homeland' for having been 'lucky' enough to be in Nazi-occupied territory... OK, that isn't a very good example." I stopped myself at this point. "But there's a better one if you're ready to listen to me for a bit."

I looked around and hearing no objections, I continued.

"Remember when I flew to the Netherlands last fall with my colleagues from work? I stumbled upon a really interesting exhibit called 'The Ongoing War' at the National Archives in the Hague. It was about the challenges the country faced after World War II and it motivated me to dig deeper into this issue..."

My mother put aside the plastic bucket with the baby goats' dinner and sat down on the other ottoman next to me.

(In)visible Children of (In)correct Parents

"Welcome to Amsterdam on this very special occasion!" an elegantly dressed man proudly displaying a medal of honour hanging from a ribbon around his neck announced with a smile from the lectern in the Beurs van Berlage conference hall.

On Saturday, 2 February 2002, some 600 people, including members of the royal family of the Netherlands, the prime minister, government officials, and parliamentarians, gathered in the premises of the former Stock and Commodities Exchange built at the turn of the 20th century in the

heart of Amsterdam. Their attention was fixed on the speaker with the medal on his chest and the young couple sitting on the two chairs in front of him. The seated man was dressed in the ceremonial uniform of a Royal Navy captain and the woman was wearing an ivory silk gown with a 5m-long train, an expensive tiara, and a lace veil. She held a bouquet of white roses, gardenias, and lilies of the valley.

"Unfortunately for our English- and Spanish-speaking guests, we will, of course, be conducting the ceremony in Dutch. But it's quite simple: the word for 'yes' in English and 'sí' in Spanish is pronounced 'ja' in Dutch, so you'll have no problem understanding the most important part of the ceremony," the man who had welcomed the guests joked in English, and the audience promptly responded with laughter.

Standing at the lectern was Job Cohen, the mayor of Amsterdam. He had the extraordinary honour of officiating the civil marriage ceremony of the Crown Prince of the Netherlands Willem-Alexander and his fiancée Máxima Zorreguieta of Argentina, who immediately after their marriage became the Princess of Orange-Nassau.

"This marriage is a confirmation of your union with the whole country," Cohen continued in his native language, his words laced with hidden meaning. "You, the groom, are accustomed to your life always being public. For you, the bride, this is relatively new, although in recent months, you got a taste of what all this entails (...) We hope you will love this sometimes difficult, but at the same time wonderful land as much as you love the crown prince of this country..."

A few seconds later, with a strike of the ceremonial gavel, the mayor affirmed the exchange of their "I dos" and the hall burst into congratulatory applause.

From the historical Stock Exchange, which is now Amsterdam's version of Italian *palazzo pubblicos*, the newlyweds headed to the Nieuwe Kerk church for the religious ceremony. The 15th-century cathedral in the city's central Dam Square is the traditional site for all royal events: inaugurations, weddings, and so forth. During the religious service, officiated by Court chaplain Carel ter Linden, the couple reaffirmed their marriage vows and exchanged the wedding bands given to them by Máxima's brother.

Out of respect for the newlywed princess' roots, at the end of the ceremony, "Adiós Nonino," a melancholic but very beautiful tango by Argentine composer Astor Piazzolla, was played. He wrote it in October 1959, a few days after receiving word of the death of his father while he was far away from home. Since then, the song has become deeply symbolic for Argentinians abroad, inspiring nostalgia for their homeland.

Thousands of Dutch filled the streets of Amsterdam, waving orange flags and balloons, wearing orange-coloured crowns, hats, and scarves to celebrate the wedding of their beloved prince. Accompanied by an honour guard, the couple did a short tour of the central streets in the royal carriage before returning to Dam Square – this time to the balcony of the Royal Palace, where they finally kissed to cheers and applause from the crowd.

Willem-Alexander and Máxima looked truly happy. The only thing marring this, the happiest day of their lives, was the absence of the princess' parents. Her father was such an unwelcome guest for the Dutch it was forbidden for him to attend his daughter's wedding. Her mother also stayed away, out of solidarity with her husband. The newlyweds had to accept their absence; otherwise, their marriage may not have happened.

After falling in love and deciding to get married, Willem-Alexander and Máxima aggravated a very sore spot which had been troubling Dutch society for over half a century, since the end of WWII.

When Hitler and Stalin launched their new war in Europe in the autumn of 1939, the Netherlands had hoped to remain neutral. But the subterfuge they used to remain neutral in WWI worked only for a very short while this time around.

"My people!

"After our country, with scrupulous conscientiousness, had observed strict neutrality during all these months, and while Holland had no other plan than to maintain this attitude, Germany last night made a sudden attack on our territory without any warning...

"I and my Government will do our duty. Do your duty everywhere and in all circumstances, everyone to the post to which he is appointed, with the utmost vigilance and with the inner calmness and strong heartedness which a clear conscience gives."

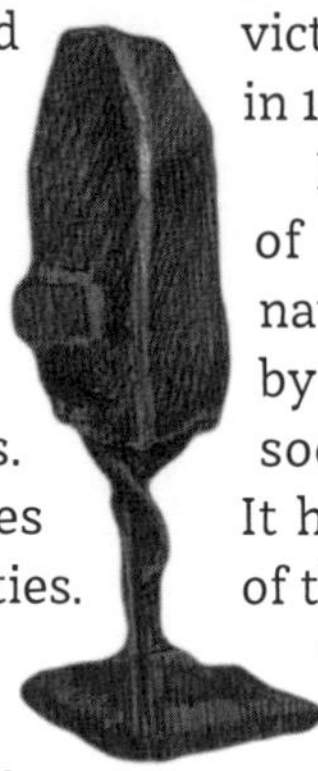

On 10 May 1940, this proclamation by Queen Wilhelmina, Willem-Alexander's great-grandmother, was printed in all the local newspapers. Early that morning, German planes dropped the first bombs on Dutch cities. This became the start of a war the country had tried so hard to avoid. The Royal Army fought back but could only hold out for several days. On 14 May, they capitulated to Nazi Germany, and two weeks later, the Reich Commissariat for the Occupied Dutch Territories was established. It would maintain control over the country until May 1945.

All this time, the queen, prime minister, and other members of the government were in exile. They managed to flee before the capitulation and rejected outright any peace talks with Germany. The rest of Wilhelmina's addresses to the Dutch people were made from London, where the BBC launched the underground Dutch radio programme *Radio Oranje*. She would speak on the radio more than 30 times during the war, and there wasn't a single speech in which the queen didn't thank the Royal Armed Forces for their heroic defence and the civilian population for their passive resistance to the occupation. This is why the Dutch often refer to her as the "mother of the Resistance" or the "mother of the homeland."

The exact number of human losses suffered by the Netherlands in WWII remains unknown. Researchers make the following estimates: 102,000 Dutch Jews and 215 Roma and Sinti were exterminated in Nazi death camps; 16,000 soldiers and 30,000 civilians died as a result of military operations; 50,000 Dutch died from health problems worsened by the war; 15,000–25,000 didn't survive the Dutch Hunger Winter of 1944–1945; 8,500 died performing forced labour in Germany; 2,000–3,000 were executed by the Nazis for being in the Resistance. This is not a complete list. In total, there were about 250,000 victims (the population of the Netherlands in 1942 was around nine million).

In the post-war period, the memory of WWII became a cornerstone of the national myth, which, like any other myth by nature, was supposed to unite Dutch society and build a sense of solidarity. It had two key elements: first, all citizens of the country, not just the Jews, had been victims of the Nazi regime; and second, all citizens of the country had united as one, risking their lives to resist the occupiers.

This interpretation of their wartime experience fuelled the belief the Dutch were "the good guys" who made the right choice in difficult circumstances. They were heroes – and beyond reproach.

Seems pretty straightforward.

This version of history wouldn't be controversial except for the overlooking of historical truths: Dutch Jews had suffered disproportionately compared with the rest of Dutch society and some citizens had supported or cooperated with the Nazis. So, not everyone in the Netherlands was either an innocent victim or a heroic fighter for liberation.

"THERE WILL BE NO PLACE FOR traitors in a liberated Netherlands," Queen Wilhelmina asserted in one of her radio addresses from London. Having learnt thousands of Dutch were suspected of collaboration, she and Prime Minister Pieter Gerbrandy set out to draft legislation for the purpose of punishing the traitors even

before the end of the war. They did this in advance, among other reasons, so ordinary Dutch citizens didn't act on their own, taking up weapons to exact fair retribution on the collaborators (although they weren't able to prevent all cases of mob justice).

Four pieces of legislation were passed in late December 1943: the Decree on Extraordinary Penal Law, the Decree on Special Courts (including Appeals), the Decree on Extraordinary Justice, and the Decree on Pardons. Together with the Decree on Political Offenses, which was passed later in 1945, the legislation formed the legal basis for the specific form of justice administered in the Netherlands in the initial post-war years, at first by the temporary Dutch Military Administration headed by General Kruls, and later by the General Directorate of Special Justice of the Ministry of Justice of the Netherlands.

It is estimated up to 150,000 people designated by this special justice legislation as collaborators were arrested and forever branded as "incorrect" Dutch. They were placed in special internment camps such as De Vergulde Hand in Vlaardingen or in existing prisons, barracks, or camps. From April 1945 to December 1948, some of the detained members of the National Socialist Movement in the Netherlands and the Dutch who volunteered with the Nazi *Schutzstaffel* (Protection Squadron — SS) and *Sicherheitsdienst* (Security Service — SD) were held in Westerbork. During the occupation, this was the main transit camp where the Nazis held Jews before they were sent by train to concentration camps in Poland, Czechoslovakia, and Germany.

There were around 180 internment camps in the Netherlands immediately after the war. Initially, former members of the Resistance served as guards. Many prisoners in these camps faced disease, malnutrition, and ill-treatment. At least 89 prisoners died in Westerbork in the first four months of their imprisonment. There is also evidence those held in De Vergulde Hand were handcuffed and chained together day and night.

Were these isolated incidents or evidence of systemic abuse? In 1947, the Parliamentary Committee of Inquiry into Government Policy during 1940–1945 was created and tried to answer that question. Two years later, Baron van Tuyll van Serooskerken, who had been commissioned to investigate the conditions in the camps for the "incorrect" Dutch, wrote in his report: "Nearly everywhere, the guards spared no effort to torture and mistreat defenceless people, using the same methods as the Nazis during occupation."

But his report came a bit too late. Most of the internment camps had closed by then. And his conclusions didn't fit with the prevailing heroic discourse in society at the time. The results of the investigation did not lead to any actions being taken by the authorities.

One hundred and fifty thousand people had been arrested. There was no way investigators, prosecutors, and judges could have handled such an avalanche of cases. That's why only a third of the potential collaborators, those accused of the most serious offenses, wound up in the defendant's chair of special courts in Amsterdam, Arnhem, Den Bosch, The Hague, and Leeuwarden. The rest didn't face charges and were released after serving several months to two years in the internment camps.

The special justice courts handed down more than 14,000 verdicts. Many of them were against Dutch members of the *Nationaal-Socialistische Beweging* (National Socialist Movement in the Netherlands — NSB), the only legal party which openly cooperated with the Nazis during the occupation. In September 1943, the NSB had almost 100,000 members.

The guilty faced various sentences, from several years to life in prison, and even execution. In 1945, the Netherlands reinstated the death penalty in order to punish those guilty of the most serious war crimes and crimes against humanity. Most of the population welcomed this decision. A former prosecutor of the Special Court in Leeuwarden later recalled in an interview:

"We were flooded with requests. We were offered gifts... in the hope we could reserve seats in the gallery. The courtrooms were packed. Sometimes you could hear the spectators shout 'Bravo!' when a death sentence was handed down."

The first official execution of a collaborator in the Netherlands was on 16 March 1946. A firing squad executed Max Blokzijl, the journalist and radio host who was responsible for Nazi propaganda in the occupied territories. On 21 March 1952, capital punishment was used for the last time on a member of the SS, Andries Jan Pieters, and the head of the SD in Friesland, Artur Albrecht. They had both been implicated in dozens of cases of torture and crimes against humanity.

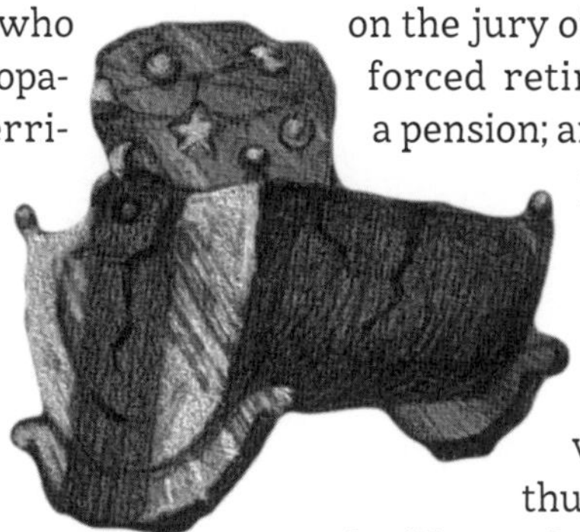

Many death sentences were later commuted to life imprisonment. Of the 145 people sentenced to death, only 42 were executed. The rest were granted royal pardons.

The only woman to be sentenced to death was Anna "Ans" van Dijk, a Jew who had been recruited by the Nazis. She pretended to be a member of the Resistance to find out where Jews were hiding and then ratted them out to the occupation administration for a reward. She was one of the most famous "Jew-hunters" in Amsterdam, responsible for betraying the whereabouts of at least 145 Jews. At one point, it was even rumoured she gave away Anne Frank's hiding place, although this was never officially corroborated. To this day, the name Anna van Dijk is associated with betrayal.

Court trials weren't the only forms of punishment awaiting the Dutch caught cooperating with the Nazis. According to a royal decree, special purification councils were established for the military, public service, police, press, business, creative professions, etc.

Some of the sanctions the purification commissions applied to collaborators included: deprivation of voting rights and bans from participation in elections; confiscation of property worth up to 20,000 guilders; deprivation of the right to hold a managerial position in any company in any business sector for 10 years; rescinding the right to claim assets co-owned with a spouse; a ban from working in journalism in any capacity; prohibition from participating in architectural tenders or being on the jury of such tenders for three years; forced retirement without the right to a pension; and prohibition from any public professional practice, including membership in professional associations, for six years.

The sanctions often came in different configurations and were in addition to internment, thus legitimising the internment itself (post factum). Between 1946 and 1950, more than 60,000 Dutch were subject to special investigations. A third of them were punished and lost certain rights.

Looking back today, some people say the Dutch policy towards Nazi collaborators was too harsh, even cruel. But those who disagree have a counterargument: it was a necessary evil and now nobody can blame the Dutch for covering up for people who were guilty of war crimes, crimes against humanity, or just being a Nazi supporter. And that makes sense. But you can find a weak spot in every assertion, and in this one, it's the children of "incorrect" parents.

"I WAS BORN IN ROTTERDAM AND was the second child of a couple where the woman was a housewife and mother, and the man earned a living designing ships. Our home faced Feyenoord Stadium, which was in South Rotterdam and was often targeted in the bombardments of May 1940. My older sister was born in February before the war. My parents had been married for almost two years at the time....

"At the moment of my birth, my father was sitting at the foot of the bed, dressed in his NSB uniform. I was literally born in

the shadow of a swastika and for years wondered how I was able to escape that shadow..."

The name of woman who wrote this is Gonda Scheffel-Baars. She was one of the first members of *Stichting Werkgroep Herkenning* (Foundation for Recognition), an organisation established in 1981 to help the children of "incorrect" parents. And, as you can see from her own words, she was the daughter of a collaborator.

Gonda's father joined the National Socialist Movement of the Netherlands in January 1942. It's difficult to say what motivated him; maybe he made the choice because he agreed with some of the German ideology. Gonda remembers him being a racist and an anti-semite who "continued to curse the Jews for years after the war." Perhaps he was tempted by the economic dividends membership in the party brought — the only political party not banned by the Nazis. When the turning point came on the eastern front and the Soviet Army began pushing German troops out of the USSR, he volunteered to fight in the war because, among other things, he was rabidly anti-communist.

In autumn 1944, Gonda's father instructed her mother to take the kids and escape to Germany. They weren't the only ones: 65,000 Dutch refugees, mostly families of NSB members, travelled there on special trains. But it didn't spare them — most returned a few months later. Some, like Gonda's mother, ended up in the Hoogezand internment camp.

Locals stood alongside the road, shouting and spitting at the women and children as they walked to the detention camp.

"They didn't ask whether the women were guilty or not, or that maybe they opposed their husbands' political choices, as my mother did, but to no avail. They didn't see us as children. If they had accepted us as children, they would have realised we were innocent because we were beyond any political choice. But the suffering of five years of occupation clouded their vision...

"This was the moment I was rejected by my own people. When I stopped belonging to the Dutch people. We became exiles, and since then I have been emotionally without citizenship, although of course I still have a Dutch passport."

Since Gonda's mother didn't belong to the party, she was released from the internment camp after about three months. While she was at the camp, her daughters lived with her sister in Amsterdam. They were lucky; if both parents had been accused of collaboration, the state would have taken the girls into custody. The Bureau for Special Youth Care in the Ministry of Justice of the Netherlands administered the policy. From 1944 to 1945, 20,000 children of interned persons were separated from their parents: 8,000 went to children's homes and 12,000 were placed with foster families.

Gonda, her sister, and her mother were taken in temporarily by relatives; first by her grandmother on her father's side, and then, reluctantly, by her mother's parents. Her father was given a relatively short sentence for membership in the NSB and for making negative comments about Queen Wilhelmina. His imprisonment was further shortened through amnesty. He was released in August 1948. The family was reunited, but her parents' marriage had been ruined, "like many marriages after the partners hadn't seen each other for years."

They moved to a small village where nobody knew about their past and her father could find a job more easily. The daughters went to school. That's where Gonda learnt "what the letters NSB meant and why we shouldn't talk about certain things. It was then I learnt in history class about the 'heroes of the Resistance and the bad guys who betrayed the country.' And I realised my father belonged to the latter. Before, we had been silent around others because we were afraid to say something 'forbidden.' But now we knew the reason why it was forbidden. Now we remained silent consciously. We were afraid we would be rejected, like in Hoogezand. We isolated ourselves..."

Poor living conditions due to the confiscation of houses and property; money problems because of discrimination by social services, the labour department, and employers; verbal and physical harassment by relatives, neighbours, teachers, and classmates resulting in social isolation; silence and emotional detachment within families; these were the realities the children, and sometimes even grandchildren, of the "incorrect" Dutch were forced to grow up in.

Many of them never had trusting relationships with their parents or grandparents. They had fewer educational opportunities and greater difficulties starting a professional career. Insecurity, mistrust of others, and anxiety over their origins prevented them from building their own lives.

The Stichting Werkgroep Herkenning was the first organisation in the Netherlands to break the wall of silence around this issue. From 2008 to 2011, they recorded dozens of testimonies by descendants of "incorrect" Dutch, which are now available on the National Archives website. There you can find Gonda Scheffel-Baars' full story.

It took a long time for the country to reach this point. Queen Beatrix, Willem-Alexander's mother, was the only one to publicly acknowledge the stigma faced by this segment of Dutch society for the sins of their parents and grandparents. In her Christmas message in 1994, she said: "The strict image of 'correct' and 'incorrect', which so often determines our opinion of the war, is based on the past. Some made bad choices: 50 years on, subsequent generations still carry the scars of those choices."

Queen Beatrix knew very well the possible consequences of a wrong choice made in the past. The Dutch protested when she married Jonkheer van Amsberg in 1966 because he was of German descent and, more importantly, had belonged to the *Hitler-Jugend*, the youth organisation of the Nazi Party.

After Queen Beatrix's speech, the Dutch government issued the first state subsidy to support Stichting Werkgroep Herkenning. Several organisations representing members of the Resistance or other victims of WWII were against this move, but their opposition was not successful and the subsidy was not cancelled; instead, it was extended for several years.

There was even greater opposition among the Dutch when Prince Willem-Alexander announced he was going to marry Máxima Zorreguieta.

The couple met and started dating in 1999, and two years later the royal family announced the engagement of the heir to the throne. Not everyone in the country welcomed this news, since the prince's fiancée was the daughter of a former Argentine government official with a very shady reputation.

"People of the Netherlands!

"These days, I am often reminded of Hamlet's words to his best friend: 'There are more things in heaven and earth, Horatio, than are dreamt of in your philosophy.' Shakespeare couldn't have conveyed my current thoughts any better. I am in a reflective mood, as I have a daughter who was only five when I became the deputy agriculture minister in 1976. A quarter of a century later, she fell in love with your crown prince, and now I am supposed to justify myself to you..."

This is the beginning of the letter Jorge Zorreguieta sent in January 2001 to *NRC Handelsblad*, one of the most widely circulated newspapers in the Netherlands. He went on to explain Argentina was always an insane country and even though he served in a brutal regime, he was never involved in politics – he always worked for the interests of Argentinian agrarians. In short, he spent his career branding breeding bulls. That's all.

At the time, there probably wasn't a single person in the Netherlands who wasn't aware of the scandalous gossip: the father of the future bride of the Prince of Orange was accused of persecuting political opponents and crimes against humanity in his native Argentina.

Michiel Baud, a professor and director of the Centre for Latin American Research and Documentation at Amsterdam University, was commissioned by the Dutch government

in September–December 2000 to conduct a special (secret) investigation and answer the following question: did Jorge Zorreguieta have anything to do with the mass disappearances, torture, and other violence in Argentina's *Guerra Sucia* (Dirty War) in the late 1970s through early 1980s.

The military junta headed by the Commander in Chief of the Army Jorge Rafael Videla came to power in a coup in March 1976. An important role was played by the then economy minister, who was the direct superior of Máxima's father. At the time, Jorge Zorreguieta was the Deputy Secretary of Agriculture, and from March 1979 to March 1981 he was the Minister of Agriculture and Livestock.

Human rights groups estimate 15,000–30,000 Argentines disappeared during Videla's rule. Some people were unlawfully arrested and imprisoned, where they were tortured and raped. Some were abducted, drugged, and thrown from planes into the Atlantic Ocean. The fate of many victims of the military junta in Argentina remains unknown.

In Professor Baud's report published in January 2001, he writes the future relative of the Dutch royal family "spent five years in a high-ranking political post, was actively and passionately committed to a regime condemned at home and abroad for eliminating fundamental democratic rights and for mass human rights violations. It is virtually impossible Zorreguieta personally took part in repressions or human rights violations during his time in government. On the other hand, it is inconceivable he did not know about the practice of repressions and the human rights situation.

"Based on the categories used in the Netherlands after WWII to assign moral guilt, being in a senior post of the military regime in Argentina... would have been considered 'incorrect'," Professor Baud said in the report, acknowledging the outrage by a portion of the population in the Netherlands. "The Dutch 'correct-incorrect' designation is a result of concrete historical circumstances when cases of active support and cooperation with the enemy led to guilty convictions on moral/legal grounds." However, these designations "may have led to a conviction but were not applied fairly and consistently."

It would seem the report put an end to all the speculation: Máxima's father had no direct connection to the policy of state terror, so there was nothing to accuse him of. But soon afterwards, two Argentine investigative journalists published a biography of dictator Videl based on hundreds of testimonies and documents, in which they claimed Jorge Zorreguieta was one of the coordinators of the coup in Argentina. Later, as a civilian minister, he may not have known the names of specific people who were targeted by the junta, but he definitely knew what was happening. He knew about it but didn't speak out against it, and silence in these situations can be considered a crime against humanity.

In 2001, the family of one of the victims of the Videla regime filed a lawsuit in the Netherlands against Jorge Zorreguieta. It was rejected because the Dutch court didn't have the jurisdiction to hear the case.

In light of all these vicissitudes actively being discussed in the press, Dutch society split into two camps. One would assume the "correct" citizens would be against the marriage of Crown Prince Willem-Alexander and Zorreguieta's daughter and the "incorrect" ones would support it. But there were actually widely differing opinions, such as this one in a letter to the editorial board of the newspaper *Algemeen Dagblad:*

"Princess Máxima's father may not have done anything bad, but he made the mistake of being a member of an 'incorrect' government that acted wrongly. Shouldn't she, as the daughter of an 'incorrect' father, like I and so many other children of 'incorrect' parents, also bear this burden? Could she later become Queen of the Netherlands given the statement by Queen Wilhelmina? If Prince Willem-Alexander... still wants to marry this young lady... then he must also

bear this burden and abdicate in order to honour his great-grandmother..."

The implementation of the solution proposed in the letter was realistic, because some parliamentarians were against the marriage of Willem-Alexander and Máxima, and they had influence over the issue. The crown prince can't marry without the permission of the States General of the Netherlands. More precisely, he can, but then he immediately loses his right to the throne.

The Prince of Orange's choice of wife threatened to spark a political crisis. In the end, Prime Minister Wim Kok and Minister of State Max van der Stoel served as intermediaries in negotiations between the Parliament and royal family. The sides agreed Máxima's father would not be invited to the wedding, and, on 4 July 2001, the United Assembly of the States General passed a law allowing Willem-Alexander and Máxima to marry.

They were married seven months later and, in 2013, after Queen Beatrix abdicated, became the king and queen consort of the Netherlands.

Their story has a happy ending. But did it bring Dutch society any closer to reconciliation? Who knows. What we do know is Willem-Alexander's inauguration, like his wedding, took place at the Nieuwe Kerk without his unwelcome father-in-law from Argentina. We'll find out more on whether this episode will aid the search for reconciliation when on 1 January 2025, the National Archives will open access to some 300,000 files in the Central Archives of Special Jurisdiction on people who cooperated or were suspected of cooperating with the Nazis.

La fin de la naïveté

"May you not live in interesting times."

Minus the word "not," the internet attributes this quote as a curse spoken by Confucius, the Chinese sage who lived in the 6–5th centuries BCE. I'm not so sure he said it since nobody can find an original source for the quote. But at this moment, I'm not concerned with the authenticity of its origin.

One of my professors in the Faculty of History of Shevchenko University in Kyiv liked to end his lectures about the Far East's past with this quote. He repeated it many times over the years, so it's not surprising several generations of students associate it with him.

I remember contemplating the meaning of those words when I was an 18-year-young sophomore in 2008. "We live in such a boring time!" I complained about myself and my classmates. "Wars, revolutions, famines – the most horrible, but at the same time the most interesting, events that gave rise to life-altering changes for Ukrainians are in the past. We missed everything! We even literally slept through the collapse of the USSR and Ukrainian independence."

Since my first day in university, I kept hearing history doesn't allow for hypotheticals. But I was convinced if I had been born in a different time and place, I wouldn't sit by idly; I would have definitely been a participant in events like the student protests in October 1990 in Ukraine called the Revolution on Granite.

Fourteen years later, hiding from Russian soldiers in an improvised bomb shelter and tightly hugging a frightened nephew, the conversation with myself took on a different tone. *"You wanted to be in the whirlwind of events? Live in an era of change? Here you go – it's happening right before your eyes..."* Disappointed by my own helplessness and inaction, I berated myself: *"C'mon, why are you sitting here? What are you waiting for? March right out of this cellar. Go outside! Otherwise, you'll miss your chance to do something – you'll miss everything again... You're one crappy revolutionary!"*

The full-scale invasion Russia launched against Ukraine on 24 February 2022, has revealed people's true colours. The 34 days I spent under occupation in a village in the Kyiv oblast gave me another optic through which to view this war. And what I beheld finally allowed me to get rid of the naïveté about myself as well as those around me.

Now that the blinders have been removed from my eyes, the world has become black and white. People are either "correct" or "incorrect."

"Good enemies don't exist," my mother warned my neighbour, in a futile attempt to bring her to her senses. My mum said this after Lesia, for the first and last time during the occupation, handed her a six-litre pot of potatoes and asked her to cook them on our gas stove. The next day, our neighbour was visited by five "good guys."

There was no need for my mother to warn me. From day one, or rather from the first shot-up car, I had no illusions about the "poor lost guys" who "went for training and ended up in a war." The Russian soldiers came here to kill, torture, rape, and rob us, and they are committing these crimes knowingly, deliberately, and in cold blood. Because this is the only way they know how to "bring order."

But I also realised I was not capable of openly and actively resisting. Unfortunately, I don't have the courage or willpower of the students who went on a hunger strike in October 1990 on the then October Revolution Square in Kyiv to protest against the signing of a new union treaty with the occupying regime. But the people of Kherson, Nova Kakhovka, Enerhodar, Melitopol, and Slavutych – who wave Ukrainian flags as they protest against the Russian invaders – do. They have the courage to resist occupation. I simply waited for my village to be liberated by the Armed Forces of Ukraine (AFU).

On 2 April, when our guys chased the occupiers back to the Belarus border and entered my village, I had another insight. Albeit an unexpected one. I noticed Lesia didn't rush to offer the Ukrainian soldiers hot tea. She didn't even come out of her house to welcome them. That's when I realised what separates us is more than the two-metre wooden fence between our gardens. I couldn't wait for the AFU to liberate us. She, however, was probably despondent, because this time her "guys" were gone for good (at least I hope so).

"Why do you care so much about that woman and her tea?" my friend Artem asked after hearing my story. He went to the front in the first days of the war and fought in Kyiv oblast. "Marichka, lots of our own have been marking infrastructure for targeting by the enemy and giving up the locations of our military equipment. That's who you should be worried about..."

I didn't have an answer for him then, but I have one now. This story matters so much to me because I believe there must be no room for traitors in a liberated Ukraine; not for the obvious collaborators Artem mentioned, nor the less obvious.

Not for Medvedchuk and Kiva. Not for Shariy. Not for the "famous Ukrainian historian" of the National Academy of Sciences of Ukraine Petro Tolochko, who in 2005 headed the Putin Policy Party, who doesn't recognise the Holodomor as genocide and gladly participates in events with the president of Russia and the Moscow patriarch. Not for those who eight years ago broke their military oath in Ukraine's Crimean Peninsula and the Donbas region. Not for those who did so now. Not for Rubizhne Mayor Serhiy Khortiv. Not for Izyum City Council deputies Anatoliy Fomichevsky and Yuriy Kozlov. Not for the average family, the husband and wife from Babyntsi in the Bucha district, who gave the Russian invaders housing and food and directions on local roads.

Not for my neighbour Lesia. Because good enemies don't exist, and neither do innocent traitors.

It's important we have a strict and well thought out solution for how to punish collaborators. Because as the experience of the de-occupied post-war Netherlands shows, the attempt at reintegration of "incorrect" citizens can have long-lasting and sometimes unexpected consequences.

With that said, I will continue to stand my ground: Ukrainians must be ready not only to fend off the Russian occupiers, but also to confront our own compatriots who, knowingly or not, want to be occupied. We can't ignore them any longer. We did so for 30 years, naively hoping this wouldn't do us much harm. But now reality has shown us just the opposite.

An Albino Raven in the Museum of Soviet Values

Story by Viktoriia Antonenko
Illustrated by Iryna Lysenko

"OH, THAT'S PROBABLY FOR US!"

The metallic jingle of keys echoing from the first floor prompted the two elderly ladies to start struggling to their feet from where they had been sitting at the top of the stairs, gossiping. I didn't quite catch what they had been talking about, but it was usually something mundane: the garden waiting for them at the dacha, or their horrible daughters-in-law, who were ruining the lives of their baby boys. And, of course, their tiny pensions, which forced them to keep working, even in their golden age. Etc. etc. etc.

They rose quite slowly; the first leaning against the 200-year-old museum wall, and the other, pushing herself up with rough, worn-out arms using the handle of her mop.

A moment later, I came into view, emerging from the semi-darkness of the ancient vestibule. My watch said it was six minutes to 8.00am and my fitness tracker had already recorded a total of two thousand six hundred forty-seven steps. I quickly slipped off my coat, hung it on the rack in the cloakroom, then deposited the flat white I had purchased on my way to work on the counter nearby. I sprang up the stairs like a rabbit, hurrying to open the exhibit hall for its morning cleaning.

Two thousand six hundred forty-eight... forty-nine... fifty... My footfalls were silent, the sound muffled by the plush dark green carpet guiding me up to the second floor of the museum.

"You're working today? I thought it was Maryna from Archives, and here I was all relaxed, and thought we could take it easy."

One of the cleaning ladies, Nina, recognised me in the dim light softly penetrating the stained-glass window, which had illuminated my path up the stairs.

"Yes, Nina, it's me. Good morning! Good morning, Svitlana!" I ascended the last few stairs and made my way toward the entrance into the museum exhibition hall, trying to avoid the cleaning supplies scattered randomly across the floor. For someone watching my acrobatics, it probably looked like I was winding my way through an obstacle course. If at this moment a thief had burst into the museum searching for some ancient and extremely valuable treasure, according to every movie ever made, here is where he would encounter the first line of defence. The unfortunate robber would trip on the broom, knocking over the buckets as he fell backwards, spilling the water down the stairs, slipping as he struggled to climb back up the last few stairs while trying to avoid the overturned buckets rolling down causing a loud racket. To top it off, as he scrambled to stand up at the top of the staircase, he would step on the flat end of a mop, the handle would flip up and smack him in the face, giving him a black eye...

"Thank God I am not the cleaning woman on the day shift today."

I smiled at my imagined scene, but was yanked back to reality when I heard Nina speaking.

"This one's always on time, even though she lives farther away than the others," she said. Pushing a few wayward locks of her hair back under her scarf, Nina directed the remarks to her colleague Sveta, who by this time was silently getting to work, bent over one of the buckets. "I just can't remember where she comes from... Where do you live, child?"

"In Brovary," I said, running my hands along the smooth wall, searching for the light switch. I wound up having to use the flashlight on my phone to find the appropriate switches. Click, click, click – and voila! Like Prometheus, I gave ~~fire~~ light to humanity. Light, which the cleaning ladies could have easily turned on themselves, but for some reason chose to sit in the dark, waiting for someone else to do it for them.

"Yeah, I remember now. You're not from Kyiv. The ones from Kyiv take their own sweet time getting to work. And then it's a miracle if you can get the cleaning done before the museum opens," Nina fumed.

By this time, both women were swishing their mops around in their water-filled buckets.

"And today's going to be a rough day. Today everyone gets into the museum for free, right?" Sveta joined in on the small talk. Not waiting for a reply, she sighed in relief. "Thank God I don't have to work a full shift..."

One day every month, all the museums in Kyiv have a sort of open house, when the entry fee is waived. On this particular day, the museum has seven, eight, even nine times as many visitors as on a regular day. On this one special day, you can hear the heavenly saviour praised over and over again.

"Thank God I am not manning the security post today."

"Thank God I am not the cleaning woman on the day shift today."

"Thank God I am not manning the security post today."

"Thank God I switched out my shift with another fire-safety officer."

"Hallelujah, I have a sore throat and won't have to deal with the unending conveyer belt of visitors."

After working at the museum for six months I discovered I work with people who are always first in line to receive a bonus, but last in line to actually do their jobs.

This was particularly evident when searching for someone to volunteer to be the "administrator-of-the-day" during the open house. For some strange reason, the administrator position has always remained vacant, and so, other museum staff had to take turns performing the job. The hunt for a volunteer resembled the game of musical chairs we all loved to play in kindergarten. When the music started, we would run around chairs laid out in a circle in the middle of the room. As soon as the music stopped, the kids would scurry and stumble to claim one of the chairs. But there was always one kid left standing.

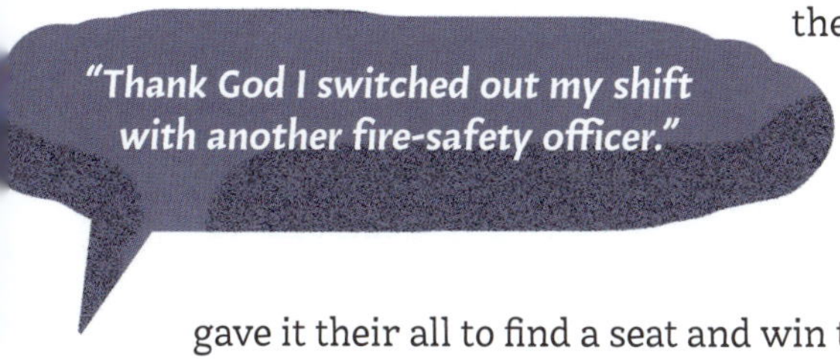

In contrast to my fellow kindergarteners, who gave it their all to find a seat and win the game, none of my museum colleagues, and there are about 50 other historical researchers who work here, wanted to sit in the chair of the administrator-of-the-day. I stood out like an albino raven among the other crows, the only one who ~~cawed~~ piped up, *"Okay, I'll do it."*

"She's batshit crazy!" The others whispered behind my back.

And that's the job I was doing today alongside Nina and Sveta.

Both cleaning women had already soaped up their mops and were waiting for me, the girl whose name they couldn't remember, to choose the proper key and open the doors to the museum. I managed to find the right key, inserted it into the lock, and paused, sharply drawing in a breath and holding it for a moment...

You see, to unlock the door on the first try was a tremendous stroke of luck. Almost like winning the lottery. Everyone in the museum knew about the tricky lock, and each one of us shared the information with the next person on duty, hoping someday the lock would be fixed.

But this was all for nought.

Days, weeks, a month, six weeks went by – and the same administrator-of-the-day once again stood in front of the same door facing down the same tricky, broken lock. Once again wishing for good luck. Because if your luck runs out – you're screwed. This door opens the entire museum, leading the way into the exhibition halls laid out one after another in a big loop. If this door isn't opened, there is no way to reach the remaining 15 doors hidden on the other side. The longer you struggled with the lock, the less time there was to clean the premises before the first visitors arrived. In other words, this was a disaster in the making...

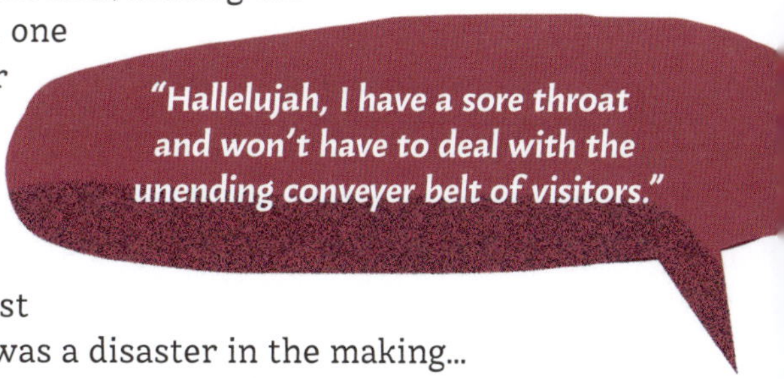

"Maybe the tricky lock is there for a reason? Part of the anti-theft system acting in concert with the buckets and mops?" I thought to myself.

"Yesterday, Karinochka had to ask the security guard to help her unlock the door. Vadym's on duty today. He's useless," Nina said.

The women stood, shifting from one foot to the other, talking to each other as if I wasn't there.

"Yeah, that one won't pick his ass up off his chair for anything," her accomplice agreed, glancing at me over her shoulder.

"If anything, maybe she could ask the fire-safety officer for help."

"Don't jinx it. Maybe she won't need any help... Maybe she's got the magic touch."

Ignoring the verbal ping-pong behind my back, I took in another big breath, like a deep-sea diver preparing to take the plunge, and rotated the key – click, click – then twisted the doorknob and triumphantly pushed the door open. *"Whew!"* I let out my breath and stepped across the threshold.

There is something elusive, an almost magical feeling, in meandering through an empty museum in the morning before the crowds of visitors invade the space. You open all the doors, turn on the lights, and draw the curtains to let in the light. Next, you check to see if all the exhibit pieces are in place, pausing along the way for a few seconds in front of your favourite painting, the portrait of a beautiful stranger in a dark blue dress with a sheer golden wrap draped around her shoulders, mentally wishing her *"Good morning, beloved,"* before you move on to the next room. The old parquet floor creaks beneath your feet and every step echoes back at you in the vacant hall. For a few brief moments, you are one-on-one with history, waking it from its slumber. Slowly, quietly, and gently, like your mother used to wake you for kindergarten and later for school.

"Antoniiiiina!"

I was already running down the stairs when the silence was pierced by the stern voice of the security guard calling my name from the first floor. My father would use the same tone when he wanted to talk to me about a bad grade for conduct from the homeroom teacher on my report card.

"Why is this happening to me? Of the four policemen who take shifts as security guards at the museum, how did I end up getting this one? It can't get any worse than this..." These were the thoughts rolling around in my head as I waltzed up to him in the entrance hall.

"Here I am!"

"There is a truck by the gates, they say they have a delivery for tomorrow's event."

Having a conversation with Vadym is like playing Russian roulette – you never know if the gun will go off when you pull the trigger while pointing it at your temple. The looming, two-metre-tall man wearing a bullet-proof vest on top of his police uniform, with a holstered weapon on his belt and accusation in his tone, grumbled: "Nobody told me anything about it."

"Should I let them in?" he added after a short pause. I readied myself to take a bullet to my head.

"Me neither. I don't know anything about it," I said. I heard the faint trembling response, as if from a great distance. *"Is that my voice?"* Under his penetrating gaze, I had shrunk down to the size of Thumbelina, craning my neck to look up at the guard and feeling cowed by his Mount Everest-sized enormity.

Remembering the schedule of events for the week was supposed to be on the administrator's desk, I grew back to my full human height of one metre sixty-eight-centimetres. *"Let's see, the journal of opening and closing the exhibits, the journal of excursions, the journal with the workers' schedules, the journal containing the reports of the person on duty... Aha! Here it is at last!"* The most important things always get lost under a pile of rubbish.

Throwing my coat over my shoulders, I made my way over to the truck, scanning the list of events as I walked. The driver was standing next to his vehicle parked at the gate leading to the museum parking lot, smoking.

"Good morning! Are you from the children's architecture festival?" I called out as I approached him, still a few metres away.

"Yeah, hi." He waited until I had come up closer and exhaled, blowing a cloud of cigarette smoke right in my face.

"Probably. I don't really know. But if that's what's written down there, then yeah. They gave me this address, told me to drive here this morning, and unload the truck. I didn't get any other instructions." He continued, unperturbed, as I coughed up my lungs. "You gonna open the gate or what?" He threw the cigarette butt on the ground nearby and started pulling himself up into the cab of the truck with his nicotine-stained fingers.

"Have another smoke. I need to check on something," I shot back. Turning away, I walked toward the museum, imagining myself forcing the driver to stuff his cigarettes down his throat. Together with the thousands of cigarette butts scattered in a thirty-metre radius around the museum.

No one likes phone calls or messages first thing in the morning, but I was left with no choice.

"@Artem, are the pieces for the architecture fest supposed to arrive today? Because there's a truck waiting outside," I wrote in a work chat with the hope my boss wouldn't tell me to go to hell in the public chat shared with all the other employees if my message woke him up.

Leaning against the railing on the porch in front of the museum, I kept checking my phone every thirty seconds. *"Sure, I'm the only one who replies to messages right away,"* I thought, angry at myself for being that way. Time crawled by at a snail's pace. It seemed as though I could have already driven over to Artem's place all the way on the other side of town in Poznyaky, gotten the answer to my question, come back, and I still would have had no reply to my text.

"So, what's going on?" the driver pushed, trying to speed things up. He had managed to run out to buy an "expresso" and smoke two more cigarettes before Artem finally replied: *"Yes, I forgot to tell you. Sorry."*

Gathering all my courage, I peered into the one-and-a-half by one-and-a-half-metre closet serving as the security post.

"Vadym, can you please open the gates? The truck *is* here for us."

"Do I look like a doorman to you?" asked the guard, without taking his eyes off the simulated tanks lined up on the screen for an attack.

"No, of course not. But you have the remote that opens the gate to the parking lot, and I don't." His feigned indifference didn't fool me for an instant. The gun was once again pressed against my temple. A cold shiver ran up my spine.

"It's not my problem. Tell the director to give the person on duty a remote," Vadym paused the game and turned his attention to me.

"But I need to let the truck in right now, and the director won't be here for two more hours," I said. I could practically hear the click of the safety on the gun coming off, got weak in the knees, and leant against the door jamb.

ЗАНАДТО

"I don't have a copy of the work order saying there was supposed to be a delivery today."

"It's not my fault. I'm sure the secretary faxed the instructions to the police station and they simply forgot to give you a copy."

"I don't care about the details. I'm telling you again, there is no work order..."

"Pleeease! I'm just trying to deal with the situation at hand..."

"If anything goes wrong, it's going to be your problem," the guard grumbled, and, taking the remote out of the drawer, tossed it at me like he was flipping a coin in a beggar's cup to rid himself of a nuisance.

"Thanks," I rasped through clenched teeth, and added to myself, *"Jerk."* I didn't have the guts to say it out loud. The day was just beginning – it was too early to piss off someone whose help I would likely need at some point in the day.

Ultimately, I survived the encounter with Vadym, alive and with the remote in hand. Hurray!

I opened the gate, let the truck into the parking lot, showed the driver where to unload the contents, and returned to the museum hall.

Today, my workplace is here.

Today, I am the person in charge. I open and close the exhibits. I welcome and speak with the visitors. I coordinate the visitor guides. I am the Queen of the Muuuuseeeeuuum!

These tasks are usually performed by a full-time administrator. But not in my museum. In my museum, they are done by historical researchers. Taking turns. Today it's my job, tomorrow, someone else's, day-after-tomorrow – a third person, and the day-after-the-day-after-tomorrow, a fourth person will be assigned to do this job.

In this place every one of us is ~~President, Queen of the Museum~~ an administrator.

This means tomorrow, the administrator-of-the-day will welcome the visitors with a smile, advise them on which excursion is most appropriate for them, and tell them about the upcoming museum events for the week. On the day-after-tomorrow, not wanting to interrupt the conversation they are having on their mobile phone, the new administrator-of-the-day will wave off visitors like buzzing flies, and the day-after-the-day-after-tomorrow, the next one won't even acknowledge the visitors, not bothering to look up from the detective novel written by Dontsova they are reading.

What can you do? It's simply human nature.

"Do you know how much was budgeted for the position? Half the salary of a historical researcher! Where am I supposed to find a normal person to work for that kind of money?" The director shot back when the griping about the situation came to a head. *"Maybe I'll redirect some of your bonuses,"* he would suggest, and after the proposal, nobody else brought up the need to hire a permanent administrator.

I sat down behind the administrator's desk. My watch said 8.37am, my fitness tracker had recorded four thousand two hundred twenty-seven steps.

Sipping the cold coffee I had successfully forgotten about, I perused the list of excursions for today. Twenty-eight! Starting from the moment the museum opened at 10.00am until 4.10pm, when the last tour was scheduled, with barely 15 minutes between each new group – and that was when we were lucky. For one class of schoolchildren, only five minutes separated the start of the tour for each group.

"Uh-oh, this is going to be great!" I thought, sarcastically, while conjuring a scene from *Braveheart* in my imagination, in which mere handfuls of Scottish farmers, armed only with pitchforks and axes, face off against the unending hordes of English horsemen and foot soldiers armed to the teeth pouring forth onto the field of battle.

Except in my head, the army of King Edward I, known as Longshanks, was made up of schoolchildren. A mixed bag of fifth, eleventh, second, third, ninth, and seventh graders. I could hear the rattle of weapons against their armour, the thunderous sound of the horses, the rhythmic marching of professional soldiers, and... I wondered whether I had made the right decision to engage in this battle.

When they are spread out over time, it's not bad. But when you have a hundred kids are all crammed together in a limited space – watch out! Walls that have withstood revolutions and wars begin to tremble in the presence of these kids, and the paintings sway back and forth in rhythm with their tremors.

Fortunately, this event happens only once a month – on the last Tuesday, when the museum doesn't charge admission, and schoolchildren arrive by the busloads. Some groups are entering the museum, while others have completed their visit and are getting ready to leave – but all the kids end up in the great hall, where it's not the battle for life, but for death that begins.

For this reason alone, the search for a volunteer to take on the administrator job on this specific day is extremely difficult. *"You simply have to survive it,"* my colleagues repeated like a mantra. But what I heard was: *"Three hundred well-armed cavalry! We are doomed..." "So many! I didn't come out to fight so the nobles could own more lands so I could work for them." "Nor did I! That's it, I'm done, boys. I'm not going to fight for them. Let's go home..."*

"That's not how it's going to be!" William Wallace's courage flared up inside me. *"You can be ready for anything – even the end of the world!"* I valiantly threw my empty paper coffee cup into the wastebasket and decisively strode over to the children's centre, keys in hand. *"Not much to choose from..."* Evaluating the scant potential of the room the museum called a "centre," I already knew what I had to do. Three minutes later, I was standing in front of the door leading to the firefighters' post.

Yes, you heard right – firefighters.

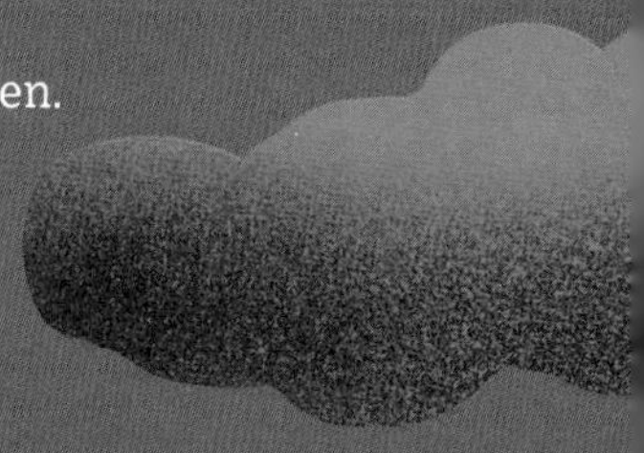

In a museum with no administrator, we had four firemen. Their main function was to watch over the fire alarm, which went off at the first sign of an emergency. After deciding if this was a real emergency or not, they would then get in touch with the local emergency services station and confirm or call off the deployment of the actual fire brigade.

In all my time working at the museum, I heard the alarm go off only once. There was no fire – thank goodness – but the fireman on duty at the time, the old-timer "uncle" Kolya, couldn't turn it off. *Woo-woo-woo...* it wailed for about half an hour. "What do you want from me?! God have mercy!" his arms akimbo, the husky, well-past-his-prime man yelled at the alarm until he was red in the face. Obviously, after the Biblical Great Flood, which he had managed to survive alongside Noah, Kolya didn't expect to have to face any more challenges from God.

Most of the time, though, the firemen spent their days listening to *chanson* (Russian pop music), playing Solitaire, and drinking alcohol.

Knock-knock! – Silence. Another knock-knock, this time louder, still producing no response. Knock-knock-knock-knock-knock-knock! I banged on the door with all my might. Little time remained to enlist allies, bolster their fighting spirit with

inspiring speeches, and ready ourselves for battle. I heard a high-pitched creaking and the door cracked open, revealing "uncle" Kolya's wrinkled visage.

"Good morning! I really need your help..." I said hastily. And would have continued at the same speed, but I noted the person on the receiving end of my words hadn't completely tuned in yet.

"Hello..." the overpowering scent of sweat, boiled eggs, onions, and ale wafted my way.

"Uncle Kolya, I am on duty today and we're expecting a lot of visitors. Please, I need your help."

I found it necessary to take a step back to avoid the aromas assailing me, threatening to disable me, the only brave heart organising the defence of the museum.

"What do we have to do?" the man asked with zero enthusiasm, yawning and scratching his head. And one more step back for me.

"We need to move the tables. Well, and move a few benches into the hall..."

"Ehhh, but what about my bad back..."

"I understand, but you won't be carrying everything by yourself."

"Who's the security guard today?"

"Vadym."

"Oh...Okay, so who's going to help me?"

"Me!"

"Aha, great. Give me five minutes, I'll meet you downstairs in the hall."

While grabbing the fourth table and carrying it out of the children's centre into the hall, the fireman directed his complaints to the back of my head: "I didn't take a job here to move furniture."

"And I thought the position of historical researcher meant I would be doing research. But the two of us understand no such official position as 'mover' will ever be added to the list of employees at the museum," I said while carrying the front end of the table, guiding it into place. "Here we are. Let's put it down."

"Is this it?"

"No, Uncle Kolya. We need some chairs, about twenty of them. Bring them out and put them here."

"You're kidding me!" sputtered the old man, massaging his arms.

"Come on, please... I would carry them here myself, but I still have to check if the elevators are working. And if the bathrooms are clean, and if there's toilet paper. And put some activities out for the kids... The exhibit guardians will be here soon, and I must assign them to their rooms..."

"Fine, fine... you've talked me into it. I'll do it, but only because you remind me of my granddaughter Virochka. She's always so annoyingly full of energy, too..." His last words were mumbled under his breath, as he shuffled his feet back toward the children's centre.

I threw out a "Thank you!" to the fireman while rushing toward the administrative side of the building, where all the museum departments were located and, in particular, the exhibitions department, which housed my command-and-control centre.

9.14am and six thousand eleven steps.

Just my luck, the office printer clunked and squealed in agony, stubbornly refusing to print the colouring pages for the kids. My defence strategy was in danger of complete failure.

"Please tell me you haven't caught the 'I don't want to work' virus. I know it's hard not to get infected in this place. C'mon, please, please, pretty please!" I danced around the printer pleading with it as if it was alive.

When after the third system reboot the piece of equipment still failed me, I closed my eyes for a second and took in a deep breath. Unfortunately, this simple breathing exercise didn't calm me. Instead, I imagined swinging an axe at the useless piece of plastic with all my might, pummelling, chopping, and essentially obliterating it – and I couldn't get myself to stop.

I would have reduced it to rubble, but the printer's imaginary execution was interrupted by the ringing of the land line.

"Hello," I answered the phone, miffed the call had cut short my revenge upon the printer.

"Tonichka?"

"Yes."

"Tonichka, we're all here already in the entry hall, we're just waiting for *you.*"

I recognised the insincere, cloyingly sweet voice of the head exhibit guardian. For thirty years, she had worked as the headmistress of a school and had never gotten used to not being in charge – to this day, she was still bossing people around and was known at the museum as the "crazy empress."

"I'll be right there, Oksana Yuriyivna. I'm already on my way!" I said. Rudely awakened from my flight of fancy, I tried one last time to get the printer to work.

Either in response to my pleading, or in fear of the repercussions, the printer, as if exorcised from evil spirits, finally began spitting out sheet after sheet of the desired documents.

One... two... three... When you're in a rush, everything around you seems to deliberately move in slow motion.

I added one hundred twenty more copies to be printed, hit "Enter" and took off like a bat out of hell back to the hall.

The time had come to divvy up the museum's "guardian-grandmothers" into the different exhibit rooms. They are the ones who are supposed to prevent visitors from touching the paintings with their greasy fingers or breaking the stained-glass windows by bashing into them with their heads. This was one more morning ritual allotted to the administrator-of-the-day, me, and so I ascended the stairs to the exhibition hall again and handed out assignments to the guardians, each one signing for the room under their care.

"Good morning! You're assigned to the first room, sign here," I presented the journal of openings and closings of the exhibits, offered a pen and indicated where to sign. "Thanks and have a great day!" I repeated fifteen more times, only changing the room number, and just as many times I heard their reply, "And I hope you have a pleasant shift!"

"It will be pleasant, if you don't grab or smack the kids' hands away and won't interrupt the museum guides to put in your own two cents." Vitriol was on the tip of my tongue.

"You have reached your goal of eight thousand steps," the fitness tracker vibrated on my wrist.

Colouring pages were laid out on two of the tables, on the third, the game "Memory," and on the fourth, puzzles of the most popular paintings in the museum. I had gathered everything which could ~~scatter the enemy soldiers~~ disperse the kids into every available corner and halt their rampage while they waited for their activities.

One last stroke to complete – the sharpening of two hundred colouring pencils. As I was leaning over the bin trying not to make a mess, two buses full of kids drove up to the front gate.

In an instant, my sense of confidence at having been prepared for the avalanche of children evaporated and was replaced by panic. Seven minutes to 10.00am. The first visitors are on our doorstep, but neither the cashier, who hands out the free tickets and takes payment for the excursions, nor the coatroom staff, nor the museum guides have shown up to the museum. *"Maybe I didn't see somebody come in when I was upstairs in the exhibit,"* I thought, dialling the number to the excursions department. The phone was answered on the first ring, but I was not comforted by the conversation.

"Alina? Super! Glad you're here. You can come down now, your first group has arrived," I said.

"Okay. But the excursion starts at 10.00am, so I'll come down at 10.00am," Alina replied.

"But I could really use your help now. The cashier and coat check are running a bit late."

"It's not my problem," and then – she hung up on me.

Picking my jaw off the floor, out of the corner of my eye, I spotted the cashier running toward the museum entrance, out of breath, looking over her shoulder at the schoolchildren pouring out of the buses, trying to outrun them.

"Good morning! Welcome to the museum! Please pay for the excursions at the cashier's desk, and for now have the children hang their coats here," I greeted the teachers from behind the counter of the cloakroom, waving my arms about as though I was directing traffic at a busy intersection.

"Jackets, hats, backpacks, water – boys and girls, leave all of those here. Don't lose your numbered tags. The bathrooms are downstairs. Who's ready to go on the first excursion – raise your hands! One, two, three... fifteen – the first group is ready. Here's your guide – Alina Olehivna! Follow her up to the second floor. You'll get to know each other better up there."

The biggest challenge in this whirlwind was for the children to hear you. As a rule, the teachers would help organise the schoolchildren. Although occasionally it didn't work out. I was especially grateful to the teachers here today, who quickly split up the children into groups to avail themselves of the three different activities on the tables.

"You shouldn't have given them the tags! They'll lose them," the coat check clerk Laryssa screeched from the entryway. She was ten minutes late for work and didn't even consider apologising or thanking me for doing her job.

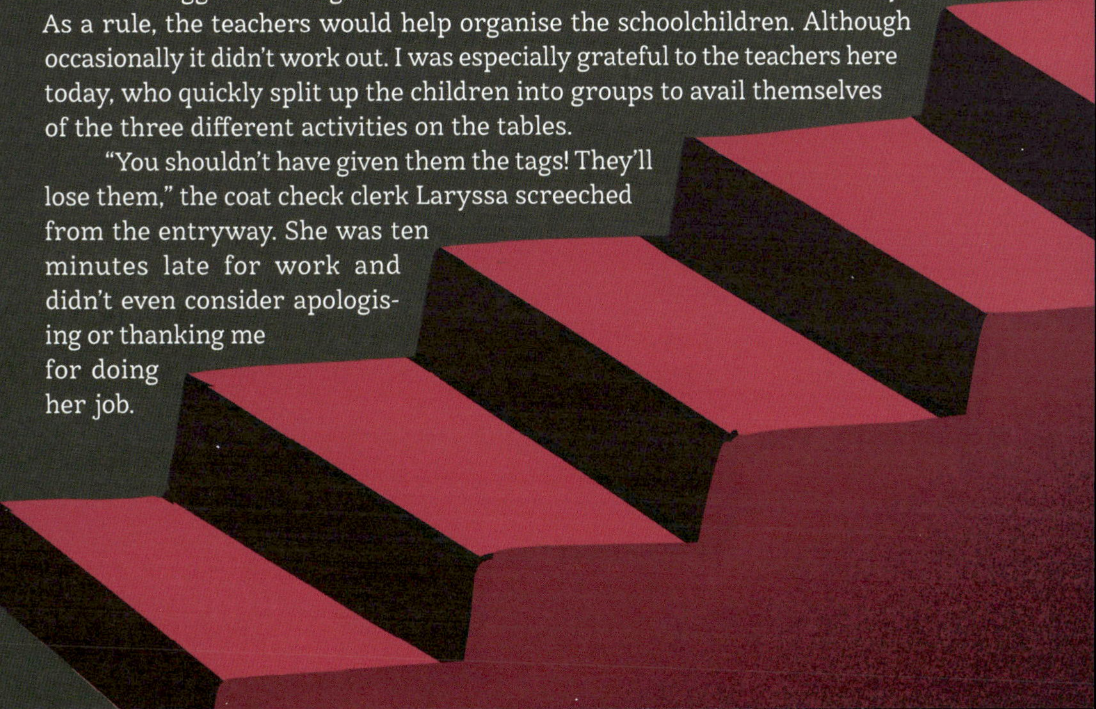

In my imagination, I was halfway along the path to the administrative office to pick up the axe I had left by the printer.

"Antonina, why is it so messy in the hall?" Rather than wishing me "Good morning," another accusation was flung in my direction. This time from Olha Victorivna, the deputy director.

"I'll ask the cleaning lady to come down. The children tracked in some mud with them from the street."

"I certainly hope you had them put on shoe covers, so they wouldn't drag mud all over the exhibition!"

"The cashier is supposed to hand them out."

"True, but you are in charge today. It's your responsibility!"

"Responsible for shoe covers! What wonderful career advancement!" I was shaking with rage inside. But it was easier to have the forty-five third graders who were colouring and building the puzzles put on the shoe covers than it was to argue. The main thing was to stop myself from stuffing the shoe covers down the deputy director's throat.

"Why do you get so upset, Tonya? There was a nervous, temperamental woman who worked here before you did, and she ended up losing her mind..." one of my older colleagues noted with feigned concern as she nonchalantly walked by, apparently unaware I was dead on my feet. Yuliya's grim experience of being taken straight from her desk as administrator-of-the-day to a psychiatric hospital four years ago, after experiencing disorientation, delirium, and hallucinations on the job, did not engender empathy in the rest of the museum staff. Instead, it convinced them conscientious work never leads to anything good.

There were occasional ten-to-fifteen-minute pauses in the flow of visitor groups. During the breaks I shuffled among the tables, laid out colouring pages, rearranged the scattered pencils, and sharpened the broken ones. I picked up the pieces of torn shoe covers the kids had not managed to throw away. And on top of all that – I was opening the gate to the parking lot, letting the school buses in and out. Anything so as not to distract the security guard from his engrossing video game.

"Remember the saying: the best workhorse on the collective farm will never become the director?" some well-wisher commented with a laugh.

11.47am and almost twelve thousand steps. One hundred twenty kids behind us, and the first visible outward sign resulting from the open house – a nervous tic in my left eye.

"The visitor is a client of the museum. They should be treated kindly and with a smile," echoed in my head. When I had just started working at the museum, I couldn't understand why you would have to codify something so obvious in the employee manual.

Several months passed by, and the reason became crystal clear. *Everything* needs to be set down in writing. For example, the administrator on duty must welcome and part company with each museum guest with a friendly greeting and goodbye. You can't condescend to the visitors, raise your voice to them, disrespect them, or insult them. It is rude to ask a disabled person *"Should I open up the handicapped bathroom?"* Because if anything, even the simplest of rules, is not written down in an official document – of course with the director's signature and the official stamp of the museum – nobody will lift a finger.

Throughout the day, I compiled a list for my firing squad.

The first one on the list was my colleague who condescendingly told me, *"I am a senior researcher, and not a clown in a shopping mall! I'm not obligated to entertain schoolchildren while they wait for their excursion. And seriously – a museum is no place for children."*

"The excursion is scheduled for 2.30pm? Let them wait! It's not my fault they can't plan their schedules properly and they arrived earlier," another one told me over the phone, out of sight.

And the third one almost killed me with the phrase *"Who said it has to be* me *who should lead an unplanned excursion? What am I – the lowest one on the totem pole here? Get someone else to do it."*

After each of those inspiring conversations, smiling became harder and harder. The realisation that only three, five, or a maximum of ten out of more than a hundred museum staff are on the same wavelength as you, is truly demoralising. And, bit by bit, you begin to have doubts. Your brain projects a PowerPoint presentation into your head with phrases heard during the day written in bold black text:

"Nobody will value what you do or thank you."

"You only get the minimum amount of work for minimum wages."

"This is not in my job description."

"I won't get a bonus anyway."

"What, am I the only one who can do this job?"

The time on my watch was 3.45pm, and on my fitness tracker – nineteen thousand eight hundred fourteen steps.

With a dark cloud hanging over me, I was counting down the minutes to the end of my shift. The weather, it seems, was synchronised with my mood. The wind picked up. Ominous grey clouds filled the sky. Rain spattered on the windowpanes and threatened to transform into a downpour.

"This was the only thing missing," I would have responded on any other day, but not today. Today, the rain was almost a relief, extinguishing the fire burning inside of me.

Precisely at that moment, I heard a door slam. The director stormed in from the administrative wing, moving toward the exhibition hall. A drop of water plunged from the ceiling landing smack onto the middle of his bald pate.

"Tonya! Do something about this!" Little did he know he had just dumped fuel on a bonfire.

"What do you suggest? You want me to do some kind of voodoo? A rain dance to stop the rain? Maybe help you wipe your bald head?" I mumbled under my breath, although my body's muscle memory already had me carrying over a clear plastic bucket to the spot where the offensive raindrop had made its assassination attempt on the director.

And one more bucket to another spot where it was dripping.

And another. And another.

And another.

For dozens of years, the museum roof had been like a sieve, and they had still not managed to repair it. However, they had managed to draw a map of all the spots where the roof leaked and purchased the same number of plastic buckets. The buckets were no longer wooden or metal – at least some progress had been made. Although in a downpour, like we had now, the buckets wouldn't suffice. Five minutes later, the museum looked like a waterfall.

Standing ankle deep in water, I phoned each of the departments, calling on my colleagues to come to the rescue.

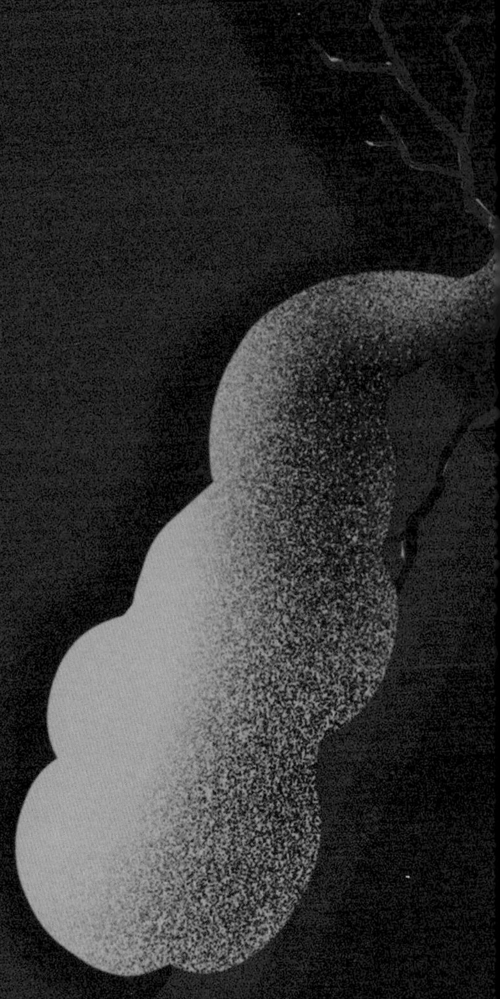

"What, it's flooding there for you?"

"Yes, it's flooding. But it's not for *me*, it's for *us*. *We* have a flood. I don't want to disillusion you, but you work in the same museum as I do. So, find some pails or buckets because I'm imploring you to bail the water out of our mutual boat," I snapped at my colleague, not bothering to hide the anger in my voice.

I was exhorting them, but, honestly, I didn't expect it to work. Because there are no written instructions in the employee manual for *"What to do in case of a flood in the museum."* And I understood perfectly what it meant in practice.

Dumping the water from the buckets into the toilet, drained of all strength, I sat down on the toilet seat, smiled crookedly and... howled with hysterical laughter.

Zones of Alienation... and Rebirth

Story by Mary Mycio
Illustrated by Maryna Lutsyk

In Memory of Mary

I am too far away from what I love and my distance is without remedy.
—ALBERT CAMUS

RARE IS THE BUREAUCRACY THAT speaks poetically and profoundly. But the name "Zone of Alienation" bestowed by Ukraine's government on the radioactive no-man's land surrounding Chornobyl was inspired. It is an evocative word for withdrawing or separating a person's affections from an object or former attachment, estrangement. In the 1970s, the *Dictionary of the Ukrainian Language* defined alienation as: "To cause the termination of a close relationship with someone; to make someone alien, distant." What could more provoke a desire to stay very far away than what remains today – even after Fukushima – the worst civilian nuclear disaster in the world?

When this story was written in April 2022, it was going to commemorate the 36th anniversary of the Chornobyl disaster by comparing the original "Zone of Alienation" with the zones created after Putin's "hybrid" war in 2014, especially the so-called "republics" in the Donetsk and Luhansk Oblasts. There is no poetry in their name: Temporarily Occupied Regions of Donetsk and Luhansk Oblasts, or the Ukrainian acronym *ORDLO*. Unlike Ukraine's Crimean Peninsula, whose population didn't change all that much – with Russians replacing any Ukrainian citizens who fled – the occupied lands in the east seemed like Chornobyl's writ large.

But when, in one of the first acts of the war, Chornobyl became a key axis for the invasion of Russian troops from Belarus into Ukraine, zones of alienation have acquired entirely new realities and meaning. After Russia captured Chornobyl and "the Zone," it seems even more symbolic that "alienation" is also the legal term for taking property away from someone. War is alienation in the extreme.

WHEN THE SOVIET UNION'S V.I.Lenin nuclear power plant exploded in 1986, and burned near the obscure town of Chornobyl about 100km north of Kyiv, invisible, deadly, and frightening radiation spread around the globe. But the worst contamination was in the areas immediately around the plant in what was then the Ukrainian Soviet Socialist Republic as well as Belarus, and, to a lesser extent, Russia. Over the earliest days and weeks, 116,000 people were evacuated from the immediate area, leaving their lives behind forever. Typically for the paranoid and taciturn USSR, everything was kept top secret. The evacuated area didn't even warrant an official name. Instead, it had numbers.

There was an outer zone, a rough circle with a 30km radius drawn around the ruined reactor building, still smouldering and highly radioactive. Informally, people called it the *trydtsiatka* meaning "the thirty" and sometimes *Zona* (meaning Zone) – though in Soviet parlance, the word usually referred to prison camps. In the early years, the area was like a prison, enclosed with barbed wire and bristling with watchtowers. Further inside "the thirty," a 10km zone surrounded the most highly radioactive areas including the plant itself and the city of Prypyat. In those days, radioactive dust covered everything, and many measures were taken to keep it from spreading around or leaving the Zone. The first time I visited in 1996, we had to change vehicles when entering "the thirty." When entering "the ten," we not only changed cars, but had to change clothes, too, to make sure we carried no radionuclides – radioactive atoms – out of the Zone when we left. Those restrictions have long been eliminated, though removing anything radioactive is still prohibited. A friend once had to leave his sneakers behind because he couldn't wash off the mud which was setting off the alarms.

From that first trip to this day, the Zone moved me in its emptiness. Perhaps it is because it echoed my own ancestral homeland Lemkivshchyna, in the distant Carpathians. Like the isolated *Polishchuky* who lived in the forests of the Prypyat swamps, *Lemkos* (people from Lemkivshchyna) also spoke an archaic Ukrainian dialect which survived in their isolated mountain tops. Their lands also became zones of alienation after the joint Polish and Soviet Communists' brutal ethnic cleansing of the Lemkos in the notorious 1947 "Action *Wisla*." It seems churlish to even mention such ancient history when Russia has been forcibly deporting Ukrainians from the lands it occupies while Poland has generously welcomed the refugees and supported Ukraine. But this complex history also makes it all the more remarkable. Most of Lemkivshchyna has long gone fallow and feral, with only the orchard trees and Cyrillic writing on some gravestones mutely testifying to the former residents. The Chornobyl Zone of Alienation is full of such abandoned cemeteries, too.

SIMPLY BY BEING "NUCLEAR," THE Chornobyl disaster touched on all the apocalyptic fears of the Cold War. It was easy to confuse with The Bomb, but it was nothing like it. For all the fears of mass deaths, the disaster killed dozens at the outset, and perhaps a few hundred over the following weeks from radiation illness. Still it became the defining catastrophe of a generation, especially in Ukraine.

In the earliest months after the nuclear disaster, when it was a massive emergency, over 600,000 "liquidators" were sent from all over the Soviet Union – but mostly the Ukrainian Soviet Socialist Republic – in tours of duty to "eliminate the consequences of the disaster." It meant to clean up the aftermath, which actually was impossible to do except for the *promzona* or industrial district closest to the reactor building, where nearly all the concrete and asphalt was excavated and replaced. But outside those areas, once man-made radiation is released into the wild, it gets into the food chain and can't really be eliminated. The best thing to do is keep it from spreading and keep people away from it. This is why, over the years, the Zone has turned into a radioactive wildlife sanctuary. Human activities are far more dangerous for wildlife than radiation, at least at the levels in Chornobyl.

Not to deny the genuine sacrifice of many, as the months wore on, hundreds of thousands were exposed to various degrees of radiation without accomplishing much at all. But it let the Kremlin pretend it was heroically "doing something." Early efforts to keep it all secret gave way under *glasnost* to glowing reports in Soviet newspapers presenting it as a battle like World War II. Someday, histories will be written to explain how those metaphors and symbolic battles from 1986 turned into real warfare in 2022 when Russian military convoys invaded the Zone in a spearhead pointed south at Kyiv.

After Chornobyl unleashed glasnost during the late Soviet years, it blew the lid off decades of secrets and lies, becoming a dramatic symbol of Soviet deceit and mismanagement. With the completion of the *Ukrytia* – also known as the Sarcophagus – to cover the reactor's lethally radioactive ruins at the end of 1986, the formal emergency had ended. But the blame of Chornobyl as the cause of many ills had only begun. When I first visited the Ukrainian SSR in 1989, nearly everyone I met had a health problem they blamed on the disaster. However, except for a real explosion of thyroid cancers, few maladies could be traced directly to radiation. The generally dismissive attitude towards health and safety that led to Chornobyl plagued all of Soviet society, and especially men.

Perhaps because of the obsessive focus on Chornobyl as a problem, it seemed Ukrainians never really accepted it as *svoye*, meaning their own. It is genuinely an alienating place in the Ukrainian psyche and identity. I shared this feeling myself in always distinguishing ChErnobyl with an E to refer to the disaster, which I considered the result and fault of Russia's policies. It was actually strange because "chErnobyl" isn't even a Russian word. I called the town and the place by the Ukrainian name ChOrnobyl. But it is a distinction without a difference now. The war has unified them. Now, I use "Chornobyl" to refer to both.

FOR MOST OF MY GENERATION OF post-war diaspora, the entire USSR was a "Zone of Alienation." Though our evenings, after school, and weekends were filled with Ukrainian choir, bandura, dancing, and Ukrainian history and language classes, few of my generation ever travelled to Ukraine. Partly, no one wanted us there. Visas were regularly denied. Besides, we were raised to see the Ukrainian SSR as illegitimate. The Communists were killing Ukraine and it was our job in the diaspora to keep the language and culture alive. Applying for a visa meant recognising its validity. So, when Chornobyl exploded, it was completely hidden from us by the Iron Curtain.

I had just moved from the homeland of my childhood, New York, to Los Angeles, where I was working as a lawyer, when the world learned of a mysterious nuclear accident in the USSR. With little news from the Soviet Union, the American press was filled with alarming speculation about dead, irradiated lands around Kyiv and a poisoned Dnipro River. It was like contemplating a moonscape, a dead zone where nothing could live. Gloomy shades of black and grey coloured my mental images. The Soviet Union had killed a piece of the earth – a piece of Ukrainian earth – before I ever had a chance to see it.

Fortunately, the most horrible scenarios turned out to be exaggerated. Ten years later, when I first went to the Zone to write a story for the *Los Angeles Times* in 1996, I was shocked to find the dominant colour wasn't grey. It was green. Amid the abandoned villages and the ghost town of Prypyat, the land had begun an extraordinary renewal – from Soviet pine plantation and potato farms to the natural wildlands of Polissia. Healthy wild boars ate apples in abandoned orchards and populations of wolves, moose, and roe deer exploded. Chornobyl's transformation into this unexpected wilderness was so surprising, most people still don't believe it to this day – especially most Ukrainians.

Indeed, after writing a book about Chornobyl and traveling there many times during the 16 years I lived in Ukraine, I noticed foreigners expressed far more interest in the subject than Ukrainians. "Why do I need it?" was a response I heard often from local friends and colleagues when I asked if they wanted to join me on my journeys into the fascinating, abandoned region. Chornobyl was a black hole. They had no attachment to it. It was a negative: a place to avoid and ignore. It barely appeared in Ukraine's culture, except for official commemorations. There weren't even many news programmes or documentaries about it. HBO's award-winning and wildly popular *Chernobyl* miniseries in 2019 was as much a revelation in Ukraine as in the West.

Such observations seemed interesting before 24 February 2022, yet seem so banal now when cities such as Kharkiv are in ruins, bombed pitilessly into rubble and ash. However, Kharkiv is still far from becoming a ghost city like Prypyat, whose entire population of 50,000 people was evacuated just three days after the disaster in 1986. At the end of March 2022, an estimated 700,000 people, about half of Kharkiv's population, still remained in the city, sheltering at home, in basements, and deep in the metro stations. Luckily, like the Kyiv metro, they were built to withstand nuclear attack. By November 2022, Kharkiv's mayor Ihor Terekhov reported the city's population had grown to 1.1 million. Kharkiv natives continue to return home, regardless of the past and ongoing damage to the city's infrastructure inflicted by Russian missile and drone attacks.

BEFORE RUSSIA LAUNCHED THE new, brutal stage of its invasion of Ukraine in February 2022, this article was going to compare the long-ago Chornobyl disaster and its depopulation of a vast territory, with the same processes in the ORDLO, where war had also driven people away, though not as completely as

radiation did. Even now, however, it is not merely theoretical. The war will also leave empty and destroyed pockets of villages, towns, and cities – some temporary, some permanent.

Of course, by nearly every measure, the war has dwarfed anything that happened during Chornobyl. The scale of suffering is incomparable. The nuclear disaster officially killed 32 people and caused about 4,000 thyroid cancers, with fewer than 10 deaths. As of November 2023, the war has killed and wounded around 28,500 civilians according to official UNHCR figures, though the actual numbers are likely much higher. Chornobyl forced the resettlement of 116,000 from the 30km zone. The war has displaced an astonishing 13 million people, including more than eight million refugees who have flooded into Poland, Germany, Slovakia, Hungary, the UK, Romania, and many other countries. Nothing like this has happened since World War II. Unlike Chornobyl evacuees, the vast majority of those refugees will be able to return home when hostilities end – if they find their homes are still standing. As of October 2023, Russian artillery and bomb attacks had destroyed more than 167,200 residential buildings according to estimates by the Kyiv School of Economics.

Even the size of Chornobyl is small compared to the ORDLO. Just the demilitarized "Grey Zone," the 400km contact line between Ukrainian armed forces and the rag tag Russian proxies they were fighting the last eight years since 2014, was much longer than anything in the "Zone of Alienation." Oddly, however, the width is also 30km. The previous front line would fit just over 13 Chornobyl Zones lined up next to each other. However, the actual interior of the so-called LNR and DNR combined is more than 16,000sq km – three times the size of all the depopulated lands around Chornobyl. Despite the differences in size, nature is likely to take over large parts of the depopulated ORDLO no matter how the fighting ends. Though it seems impossible to consider now as war rages on, when peace returns, new zones of alienation may also appear.

This may include new "Grey Zones" of constant military vigilance on Ukraine's border with Russia, perhaps with new demilitarized zones. Like the rules and regulations of the Chornobyl Zone preventing the spread of radiation into the rest of Ukraine, those boundaries will hopefully block the spread of the psycho-Soviet ideology of *russkiy mir* (Russian World), resurrected like a zombie in the Russian-occupied lands since 2014. For most of the following eight years, the tragic costs of keeping them from spreading into Ukraine were the deaths of several soldiers a week on the contact line. But after 24 February 2022, the price became national survival.

Now, the beautiful forests and wetlands north of Kyiv that were part of Chornobyl lore – like Borodyanka, where some Prypyat evacuees were first taken – have become places of horrors thought forgotten in the 21st century. Soviet propaganda presented Chornobyl as a metaphorical war against an invisible enemy. Tanks were used to bury cottages coated with radioactive dust, which might – or might not – give someone cancer in future decades. Today, it is a real war, the enemy has a face and tanks are used to kill and destroy, leaving visible wounds and scars, which will last lifetimes.

The Battles of Chornobyl

Few details are known about how the Russian troops invaded the Zone from Belarus. Its radioactively contaminated "Polissia Nature Reserve" doesn't have many roads. But there were enough to drive an army through it. You can walk to the border from the towns of Chornobyl or Prypyat. Aside from being a very direct route to Kyiv, the border had long been only minimally defended and ignored as a security issue for decades. It didn't even warrant border guards because their agency wouldn't give their personnel extra pay for their exposure to radiation risk. "Who would go there?" was the prevailing attitude about security. "Stalkers," or trespassing daredevils who went bushwhacking and avoided the necessary permits, posed the biggest problems.

In February 2022, Ukraine suddenly made a show of beefing up defences there and practicing urban warfare in the abandoned ghost town of Prypyat. More worryingly, it closed the Zone to tourists for two months. Evidently, US government eavesdropping on Russia's Chechen mercenaries revealed the Zone's coming role in the war. It was truly hard to believe. But at the time, I didn't think Putin would invade further, which worried me because I had been equally convinced – and equally wrong – he wouldn't invade in 2014. It's not clear how Ukraine prepared to defend the Zone.

The 24 February 2022 invasion came in two columns, according to Zone expert Denis Vishnevsky's post on Facebook. One of them took a small road from Belaya Soroka on the Belarus side of the border into Benivka northwest from the ghost town of Prypyat in Ukraine. The road was paved but very narrow and there were no physical barriers at the border. Video showed military vehicles driving off the road to pass each other in the forest. From there, it was a short route to the Chornobyl plant itself, which the invaders captured that night, taking the plant personnel and some Ukrainian National Guards hostage.

Reportedly, a stalker who had been in one of the Prypyat high rises saw the military columns and heard explosions the first night of the invasion. Based on satellite maps of small fires and radiation spikes probably caused by explosions, there seems to have been fighting. If so, the Battle of Chornobyl was one of the first ground battles of the Russian invasion. Immediately afterwards no information emerged from the Zone or its surroundings. It was deep in the enemy's rear. My Chornobyl friends on social media went silent, posting little. The military occupation of a radioactive zone could only bring bad news.

Rumours emerged the Russians might be digging trenches in the Red Forest, one of the most contaminated places on the planet, raising radioactive dust way above safe levels. Certainly, the road they took from Belarus took them right into this area. Reportedly, the troops – many from Chechnya – didn't understand the radioactive risks at all and knew nothing about Chornobyl. That made them all the easier to manipulate with scary stories about busloads of Russian soldiers being sent to Belarus with acute radiation illness. The tales were not true. Radiation levels simply are not high enough. But it may have been part of a very successful psychological operation.

On 27 February 2022, three days after the invasion, during Ukraine and Russia's first negotiations somewhere on the Belarus-Ukraine border, the Kremlin prepared its attack on Kyiv. On Twitter, a video showed a column of armoured vehicles driving down a road past the Red Forest. The distinctive white stela for the town of Prypyat stood far in the background. A soldier wearing no protective gear against radiation waved at the vehicles, as though to move more quickly. The invaders were probably heading for the Dytiatky checkpoint on the southern boundary of the Zone, in the direction of Kyiv.

Battle groups seem to have gone directly to the Hostomel airport, where they were to meet up with Russian paratroopers. Instead, Ukraine repelled them in a battle which reportedly killed Chechen Major General Magomed Tushaev. The same day, another video showed the traffic circle north of Ivankiv with the large sculpture of an egg familiar to anyone who has travelled to Chornobyl. In the distance, an armoured vehicle burned and smoked while a victorious Ukrainian soldier carrying an NLAW anti-tank weapon is filmed by his brother-in-arms who is shouting, in Russian: "Russian pederasts, die! Fucking Russian beasts. Die! For every tear drop... For every tear drop, die you fuckers!" and then, after a short pause: I fucking swear after this fucking war I will never speak Russian again, fuck! You beasts, go fuck yourselves!"

It is unclear how many troops and equipment were deployed in the Zone. It seems many of them ended up in the mysterious convoy of armour and trucks northwest of Kyiv made famous by the commercial satellite company Maxar. The column began right outside the Zone's Dytiatky checkpoint to the north and stretched south as far as the village of Zdvyzhivka, where half a dozen armoured vehicles were shown parked in early March 2022. Though it regularly seemed to change its length as vehicles moved closer and further apart, the front of the column didn't move much at all. Were they poised for the victory Putin had planned three days after the invasion? Or did someone realise Chornobyl was a radioactive place and decided it was better to leave, even if it meant burning up fuel and food as a sitting target for Ukrainian drones?

Reportedly, about 1,000 troops were in the Chornobyl plant itself, holding the workers hostage, with another 500 in the town of Chornobyl, where they looted everything including the high-tech lab for studying the unique environment. On 9 March 2022, the lights went out due to unspecified "combat actions." While the plant has been decommissioned since 2000, ventilation and other safety systems need power to protect the workers who keep the systems stable. Nuclear reactors don't just go away. More worryingly, spent fuel rods were stored in pools on the sprawling *promzona* or industrial park surrounding the reactor buildings. Spent fuel is the dirtiest part of the civilian fuel cycle, far more radioactive than fresh rods and if power is lost to their cooling water, they would burn from the residual heat. The resulting cloud could be lethal up close and spread future cancer risks with the wind in all directions – including to Belarus and Russia. Perhaps that danger made the Kremlin see sense. But somehow, without much fanfare, Ukraine reportedly restored power a few days later. Presumably, it must have been a part of the negotiations with Russia.

In the meantime, while the Russian battle groups left death and destruction in their failed assault in the Bucha–Hostomel–Irpin triangle to push into Kyiv, the mysterious Chornobyl convoy kept standing still. Was this what the Russians meant when they announced on 23 March 2022 they never planned to fight for Kyiv? They just made a giant traffic jam instead? By the end of March 2022, satellites showed trenches alongside the road, suggesting the Russians were digging in. In some places, they went into the woods. But mostly the vehicles couldn't leave the roads. Not only because of the early spring mud. The meandering Prypyat River system, created after the last Ice Age, is the largest wetland in Europe. The lands on either side of the asphalt are dominated by forests, swamps, bogs, and rivers – even in dry weather.

POLISSIA NEVER HAD GOOD FARMland. On the eve of the nuclear disaster, it was the least populated region of the Ukrainian Soviet Socialist Republic, had the lowest density of roads and, to be honest, never produced much of note in history, politics, industry, or the arts. No one particularly famous came from Polissia – except Ukraine's fabulous naïve painter, Maria Prymachenko. In the medieval times, its inhabitants were known as *Derevliany* – people of the woods – and among the founding tribes of Kyivan Rus', the eastern Slavic empire. In a 12th-century chronicle, Chornobyl merited one mention as a hunting lodge. After that, little of note happened.

But it was still the centre of the universe to those who lived there, who came to be known as *Polishchuky*. Though actually that's what outsiders called them. They called themselves *nashi* – our people. Protected by their swamps, where only experienced pilots could navigate, the Polishchuky resisted Sovietization the longest in Ukraine. They even escaped the worst ravages of the Holodomor by surviving on the fruits of the forest. They spoke an archaic dialect that they called *po-nashomu* (in our way), a seemingly vague ethnic identity that nevertheless had strict boundaries. Oddly, my Lemko ancestors also referred to their dialect of Ukrainian as *po-nashomu*, though they lived hundreds of miles away, perhaps reflecting a pre-modern self-designation before the rise of nations.

The surrounding landscapes of old forest and pine plantations made the area popular for hunting, fishing, and camping when Chornobyl's first nuclear reactor went online in 1977. Leonid Brezhnev was the USSR's increasingly incoherent General Secretary at the time. When the ill-fated fourth reactor was completed in 1983, Soviet spymaster Yuri Andropov was in charge, and when it exploded in 1986, Mikhail Gorbachev – the USSR's last leader – had been General Secretary for one year. The city of Prypyat, founded in 1970 to house the plant's workers, stood just a few miles from the plant.

Standing amid the forests like a high-rise alien ship, Prypyat was a colony of Soviet people amid the native Polishchuky in villages around them. By then, the swamps and bogs had been drained and the rebellious Polishchuky were finally cowed and collectivized into potato and dairy farms.

Moscow killed millions and then moved millions more around the vast country arbitrarily, mixing ethnic groups. Prypyat was a perfect example. Its 49,000 inhabitants were not native to the area but were sent there on *komandirovky* or secondments, which were job assignments you couldn't refuse. To this day, the older generation of Ukraine's nuclear industry is made up of the same multiethnic mix. These include the Zaporizhzhia nuclear plant workers held hostage by Russian invaders for months.

Soviet citizens were very diverse and included Europeans and Asians as well as Africans who moved there from the USSR's client states. It was all very inclusive, so long as everyone spouted the same Communist dogmas and acknowledged Russians as the superior caste. The purpose of Soviet diversity was to destroy native ethnic groups and

cultures to forge everyone into the same homogenised and Russian-speaking *Homo Sovieticus*, regardless of skin tone. In regions such as Donetsk, Moscow used huge, forced population transfers from throughout the USSR, in part to replace the Ukrainians Stalin starved in the Holodomor.

The criminally atavistic return to those Stalinist methods was first signalled in the days leading up to the full-scale invasion, after Putin recognised his fake "republics," the occupied lands in Luhansk and Donetsk oblasts on 21 February 2022. Waiting to see what the Kremlin would do next, the world watched with growing foreboding as Kremlin forces demonstratively "evacuated" busloads of women, children, and the elderly from the ORDLO into the Russian interior. The men were ordered to stay and be conscripted. Billboards on the streets compared the upcoming battles to World War II. Just a few weeks later, after the war began, a modern wave of Stalin-style deportations began in places like Bucha, where occupiers tried to force residents to evacuate to Belarus, or Mariupol, where, by the end of March 2022, 40,000 had reportedly been kidnapped and taken either into the ORDLO or Russia. More than a million people are said to have been forcibly deported to Russia. And the list of war crimes grows daily. After Ukraine liberated the small suburban town of Bucha, they found streets filled with dead civilians. The invaders murdered men between the ages of 16 and 60, and raped women and girls. They stole computers, clothes, jewellery, cash and even appliances including washing machines, then reportedly sold them in Belarusian markets or shipped them home.

Before Putin's brutal war on Ukraine, Russia's crimes against its neighbours were always hidden. The Kremlin controlled the territory where the worst atrocities occurred, like during the Holodomor and Stalin's Great Terror. There are no photographs from the Gulag like there are from the Holocaust because Nazi Germany was vanquished and occupied by the Allies while Russia never was. This is the first time the world can see Russia's brutality directly. It is one of the paradigmatic shifts of this war.

More than 13 million people – mostly women and children – have fled their homes in the first days of the full-scale invasion. More than eight million of them left the country, mostly traveling to Ukraine's neighbours Poland, Moldova, Hungary, and Romania as well as to Germany and the UK. It has been the largest movement of refugees in Europe since the end of World War II. Back then, few Ukrainians had the language skills to tell of their horrors. Today, they do and are able to tell their stories of death, destruction, and brutality.

IN THE FOURTH DECADE AFTER the Chornobyl disaster, on the eve of Russia's ruinous and murderous invasion of 2022, the "Zone of Alienation" had become a beautiful, eerie, and radioactive sanctuary. By alienating humans and their activities, radiation made it safe for wildlife. You can barely see evidence anymore of the once-cultivated fields for the wild grasses, shrubs, and trees, which have taken over the fields. It showed us how nature will renew itself and cleanse the land from what seems to be terrible injuries by humans.

Perhaps something similar will happen in some of the destroyed towns and cities after the war. I hope they all rebuild, and their people return to them to start their new lives. Hopefully Russia's frozen assets in the West can be used to pay for reparations and reconstruction. But rebuilding will take time. Some places may remain depopulated ghost towns for years. The ruins of Mariupol, Kharkiv, and Chernihiv and small towns like Bucha and Ivankiv will long remind us of what had been lost, like the empty high rises of Prypyat. We may see new "Zones of Alienation," where people won't go, at least for a while. But they will also symbolise what has been gained as "Hero Cities" and monuments to Ukraine's own Patriotic War.

Wartime destruction takes years to renew, like the very strange scheme Russian Defence Minister Sergei Shoigu announced in late March 2022 to cut down all the trees in the ORDLO – soon before suffering a heart attack, which almost proved fatal – and fated. It can take but a season to regrow meadows and fields. But trees take decades and completely natural landscapes, like the steppes in Ukraine's Donbas, take even longer.

If areas such as Ukraine's Crimean Peninsula and the ORDLO remain occupied, their populations are likely to remain far lower than in 2014, before the war began. The enclaves will be closed, like Stalin's Soviet Union. In such emptiness and desolation, nature is sure to return. It takes enormous effort to keep human spaces civilised. Otherwise, roots buckle the roads and forests grow between the cracks. Prypyat's high-rise buildings disappear amid the thick forests now enveloping them.

Before Putin's full-scale invasion, similar processes were beginning in the ORDLO. In September 2021, the video of a herd of wild boar running across a broad boulevard in Donetsk caused a minor social media sensation. It was impossible to verify, but entirely believable. In Chornobyl, wild boars were the first large animals to repopulate the Zone. Everyone there seems to have a story about meeting the wild pigs in unexpected places. But some strange species never returned, like the *rusalky* of myth and folklore. The powerful water nymphs are warded off by the herb wormwood, sometimes known as Chornobyl or, in Ukrainian, *polyn*. If radiation is like wormwood, rusalky won't return for the 24,000 years needed for plutonium to decay.

But large animals that had disappeared from Polissia for a century have filled the depopulated wildlands, like wolves, moose, and even brown bears, creating new folklore and legends. One was the story of the deadly and hungry *Korohod* Bear, which was what some Zone experts told the Russian invaders. Also, those soldiers who dug trenches in the Red Forest? They were already dying of radiation sickness in a Belarus hospital. There was even one about a mysterious Black Stalker in the woods. None of these fables were true. But they spread among the Russian occupiers. They may also have played a part in Russia's swift retreat from the northwest part of Kyiv Oblast amid rumours the troops were rebelling against remaining in the radioactive area. Chornobyl – and the Korohod Bear – may have helped stop the invasion of Kyiv.

By 31 March 2022, with shocking speed, Russia retreated from Chornobyl. Reportedly, 10,000 vehicles drove through the Zone as they fled from the northwest part of Kyiv Oblast into Belarus, taking with them some troops of the Ukrainian National Guard captured in the first night of the war. Though there were unclear rumours of some Russians remaining on the site, on 2 April 2022, the Ukrainian flag was raised again in the Zone. The next day, Ukraine announced it had retaken control of Prypyat, and parts of the border – probably, the Benivka area. Now it is in full control of the Zone, though it remains dangerous. Radiation levels picked up in some areas from getting churned by Russian invaders. But mines and unexploded ordnance are bigger problems.

The Future

Soon after the Chornobyl disaster, when I was living in Los Angeles, I had a dream. In my parents' brightly lit kitchen, the nuclear reactor core sat in the middle of the linoleum. It wasn't big, and didn't look very impressive, but I knew it was emitting deadly, invisible rays. We went about our business, pretending it wasn't there. Yet I knew it was dangerous and told my mother: "We have to get rid of this thing!" In my diaspora upbringing, America was the world outdoors, but Ukraine was in the house, and the kitchen was its centre. And my mother's very sensible response was: "But where are we supposed to put it?"

There is no place to put Chornobyl, and won't be for many thousands of years, until the most dangerous radioactive atoms decay. By that time, our languages won't even be intelligible to anyone left on earth and no one will be able to read the "Danger! Keep Out!" signs we might leave there today. Its stewards will always have to be vigilant. The 2022 Battles of Chornobyl showed the dangers of too much alienation from a big part of Ukraine's landscape. With the Crimean Peninsula or the ORDLO, it has been forgivable over the last eight years before the full-scale invasion. They are closed to Ukraine by its enemy. But perhaps losing Chornobyl to the occupier in the invasion showed its importance now that Kyiv has won it back.

For the people closest to them, Chornobyl and the "Zone of Alienation" seemed to have a certain sacral quality, kept at a distance from sinful humans. It is why no one in the rest of Ukraine really thought much about it – even as a matter of national security. And perhaps this is why it was so vulnerable to invasion. The only dangers Ukraine perceived from the Zone came from radiation, not tanks. Not until it was too late. But it exploited those radiation fears ably. Someday, we will learn more details about the Korohod Bear. Not about the animal. The brown bears exist. But how such Chornobyl scare stories were concocted and spread. This may be one of the most successful psychological operations of the war.

Until then, we all wait for clarity of when this war will end and how Ukraine will renew its destroyed areas and rebuild a unified homeland. It is worth remembering Chornobyl is not only a story of alienation, imposed by the criminal negligence of the Soviet system. It is also the story of the land's rebirth and renewal in independent Ukraine. Yes, it is dangerous and a money pit and will be radioactive for longer than any of us can even imagine. But it is also beautiful, inspiring, and magical – and will deserve a place in the Ukrainian Pantheon of Heroes after this war.

This story was originally written in April 2022, two months into Russia's full-scale invasion of Ukraine, when the situation and the future looked grim. The Zones of Alienation have now expanded physically into places such as Russian-occupied Mariupol and Melitopol and psychologically into millions of Ukrainians displaced from their homes. The battle to recapture and revitalise the Zones is still ahead, and the lessons of Chornobyl's rebirth can help guide the process.

The story has been updated with data available as of the end of December 2023.

The Curious Case of a Delusional Codependency,

or The Origins and Nature of Germany's "Special Relationship" with Russia

Story by Sergej Sumlenny
Illustrated by Oleh Smal

"DEEP IN THE SOUTH OF RUSSIA, in the heart of Siberia, the deepest lake on Earth – Lake Baikal – lies dormant this time of year."

These words introduced viewers to the documentary "Winter Trip to Lake Baikal" on Germany's most popular TV channel, the public broadcasting station *ZDF*. It's Christmas 2021 and the documentary fits in perfectly with the traditional Christmas stories aired on German television. The cinematography is excellent, as always, but the film is full of clichés reminiscent of the kingdoms in the holiday fairy tales, which will be shown on the channel after the film. There are long sweeping panoramic scenes. A train, tiny compared to the vast expanse of the icy lake and snowy mountains, chugs along the shore, its blue cars gliding under the endless azure sky creating a sharp contrast with the lily-white snow. "The lake is frozen for six months of the year. The ice cover is so thick cars can drive on it from November to May," the narrator continues. The camera amplifies his words with dramatic images, cutting to a Russian man in a fur hat, then to an old jalopy, revealing minor details of a poor but honest life lived close to nature. You can hear the sounds of an ancient truck engine trying to start: once, twice, and on the third attempt – the engine finally turns over.

The images change, staying within the confines of the sterile, castrated narrative. Snow, ordinary people saying pedestrian things, powerful primordial nature with the mise-en-scène of vast expanses, exotic cold. Simple people who live somewhere out there, so far away and so differently it's almost like watching mysterious caged birds in a zoo. This Russia, of course, cannot be compared to anything else. It is unique, peaceful, original, melodic, beautiful. One can only dream of someday travelling on this train, to meet these people, and marvel at the cold while buying their souvenirs, which, along with the help of countless photos, will remind you of this trip for the rest of your life.

Sentimentality oozes from the screen like honey from a beehive. Viewers can't help but fantasise about this once-in-a-lifetime trip. Maybe someday...

But by the time this show aired in Germany, on 25 December 2021, Russia had already deployed tens of thousands of soldiers to its border with Ukraine and was preparing to launch the bloodiest war in Europe since World War II. Neither the German public nor the German political establishment was ready to respond to this threat, let alone believe it.

Germany's relationship with Russia is the central issue influencing European and global security. Too often, Germany's foreign policy decisions are made based on a "special stance" towards Moscow. There are plenty of examples. In 2016, at the peak of the Russian occupation of Ukraine (not counting the full-scale aggression in 2022), German President Frank-Walter Steinmeier visited Yekaterinburg to give a speech at the Ural Federal University. Just a year earlier, when he was still the German foreign minister, he visited Ukraine, and for the first (and only) time travelled to the east of the country, where he saw the destruction caused by the Russian army. Steinmeier knew what the regions destroyed by Russia looked like. But in 2016, now Germany's head of state, he spoke with the Russians as if they were close friends. "His Excellency Foreign Minister, my dear Sergey," he said in the opening of his speech, addressing Russian Foreign Minister Lavrov, a rabid supporter of Russia's aggression, and subsequently offered Lavrov a full range of cooperation.

In his speech, Steinmeier mentioned all of Germany's personal and economic ties with Russia, often repeating the words "dialogue" and "understanding."

"...We must approach each other and make use of the channels we have, such as the 'Petersburg dialogue' or the summer school that is about to start here... We need to find common ground and we need to work together! This applies as much to the big issues – war and peace, Ukraine and Syria – as it does to relations between the people in our two countries... Please remain curious about each other's country and work towards a good future in German-Russian relations. That is what I ask of you."

The German president, who is the spokesperson for the fundamental values of German democracy, and former foreign minister, who should have known Russia's role in the world better than anyone, seriously suggested working together with Russia. Working together in Syria, where for years Russian aviation had been annihilating the population, deliberately attacking hospitals, schools, and civilian infrastructure. And working together in Ukraine, where Russia had occupied a large part of Ukrainian territory, kidnapping and torturing the population.

That same Steinmeier, in a February 2021 interview in the newspaper *Rheinische Post,* defended the construction of the Nord Stream 2 gas pipeline, saying Germany "owed" Russia (yes, Russia!) for German crimes committed during World War II, and should compensate Russia for its losses: namely, through the construction of the gas pipeline to transport Russian gas. Steinmeier simply ignored the protests of other countries who had suffered from the Nazis no less, and, in fact, even more than Russia – Poland and Ukraine for example – who were against building Nord Stream 2. Again, there's no way he could have pled ignorance. Shortly before the interview, he had visited Babyn Yar, the site on the outskirts of Kyiv where over the course of two days in late September 1941 the Nazis shot dead some 30,000 Ukrainian Jews. This was the largest mass murder of Jews in the Holocaust, and it occurred in this one location over a 48-hour period of time – a Holocaust before the start of the formal Holocaust. In Babyn Yar, Jews were massacred en masse even before the January 1942 Wannsee Conference and the proposal of the "Final Solution to the Jewish Problem." But neither Babyn Yar, nor the Warsaw Ghetto, nor the Koriukivka massacre (when some 6,700 Ukrainian civilians were killed in the largest destruction of a settlement during the Nazi terror), nor the quashing of the

Warsaw Uprising prevented Steinmeier from ignoring Germany's guilt towards its neighbours – Ukrainians and Poles – and singling out Moscow as the only partner to whom Germany has any obligations.

An erroneous interpretation may have led to the accusation that the German president was denying the Holocaust, when in fact it was something else – a maniacal fascination with Russia. This stance towards Russia is often associated with the Social Democratic Party of Germany (SPD), whose members include Frank-Walter Steinmeier, its infamous former party leader and patron Gerhard Schröder, as well as many other adherents of "special relations" with Moscow. But to think that would be a mistake. The unhealthy singling out of Russia in foreign policy and the prioritisation of Moscow's interests is typical of all German political parties. It's more a national position than a simple political party platform.

For example, German Foreign Minister Annalena Baerbock, a member of The Greens, the party most critical of Russia, visited Kyiv shortly before the full-scale invasion. When speaking about the potential of providing weapons to Ukraine on the backdrop of the threat of a Russian invasion, Baerbock stressed Germany will not provide weapons because it "bears a special responsibility." She meant Germany's responsibility for the crimes of the Nazis. In the German foreign minister's political and historical point of view, this responsibility extended exclusively to Russia, making it impossible to imagine German weapons could be given to Ukraine, because in Ukrainian hands they could be aimed at Russians. The German minister refused to accept the fact the Nazis had killed 16 per cent of the population on the territory of Ukraine, destroyed hundreds of cities, and deported millions of civilians to serve as forced labourers (and therefore should fulfil its responsibility to Ukraine today, when a new Russian nationalist, chauvinist ideology threatens the existence of Ukrainians as a nation). She denied support to the descendants of those whom the Nazis killed in WWII.

Of course, with time, particularly after the crimes committed by the Russians in Bucha and Irpin became known, this attitude changed. In May 2022, Annalena Baerbock visited Bucha, where the Russians had murdered civilians, and tortured and raped Ukrainian women. During her visit, the German foreign minister appeared shocked and firmly called for supplying weapons to Ukraine. German Chancellor Olaf Scholz started saying Russia is waging a war to destroy Ukraine. Other politicians, such as Marie-Agnes Strack-Zimmermann, chair of the Defence Committee in the *Bundestag*, insisted Ukraine be given nearly all available weapons as quickly as possible. The majority of the population, except for supporters of the radical right-wing party Alternative for Germany and neo-communist Left Party, also demanded Ukraine be supplied with weapons.

In the summer of 2022, Germany delivered the first powerful Panzerhaubitze 2000 howitzers to Ukraine. Soon after, the German IRIS-T high-tech air-defence missile system began protecting the skies over Kyiv. In January 2023, the German government gave in to pressure from neighbouring countries and allowed the export of Leopard 2 tanks to Ukraine. According to a May 2022 poll conducted by the Munich Security Conference, 81 per cent of Germans considered Russia a threat. The poll showed that Germans considered Moscow a greater threat than climate change and a future global pandemic. But all these changes came quite late. Moreover, the Germans' attitude towards Russia changed so suddenly in 2022 they're likely to revert to long-standing traditions once Putin's regime, which the war against Ukraine is associated with, disappears and a new regime – more pleasant and sophisticated, but similarly imperialist – takes its place.

Nevertheless, the moral blindness of the Germans at the outbreak of the war was shocking. On 25 January 2022, the

Association of Jewish Organizations and Communities of Ukraine sent an open letter to German Chancellor Olaf Scholz stating Ukraine faces the threat of annihilation, and the history of the 20th century teaches us not to appease the aggressor, urging Germany not to block the supply of NATO weapons to Ukraine. The fact Ukrainian Jews, a community almost completely wiped out by the Nazis during the Holocaust, urged the German chancellor not to obstruct them being saved from further annihilation was frightening for its inherent fear. It was hard to imagine such a letter could get no response. But not only did Chancellor Scholz not respond, he went to Moscow to negotiate a compromise with Putin. His love for Russia outweighed any sense of historical responsibility.

The Elixir of Catherine

You will often hear that Russia being treated as an extremely important partner and German hypersensitivity to Russia's interests are a result of World War II and the German people's sense of guilt for Nazi crimes committed on the territory of the Soviet Union. This is generally true. In his lectures, which are helpful in understanding the European context, historian Timothy Snyder points out Germany continues to ignore its responsibility to Ukraine and other countries of Central and Eastern Europe in favour of Russia. But if you look closely, you will see Germany's mystical fascination with Russia is nothing new: it is far more deeply rooted in the German worldview than in its post-war iteration.

There are several layers to the German fascination with Russia. One is purely material: Russia is a source of revenue and offers chances for social and economic growth impossible at home. For Germans in the 18th century, Russia became a country of endless opportunities outrivalling those in Europe.

The most famous German story of rapid career growth in Russia remains the rise of Princess Sophie Friederike Auguste von Anhalt-Zerbst-Dornburg, who went from being the daughter of a Prussian general and heiress of an old but poor family, to Russian Empress Catherine the Great – the absolute ruler of one of the largest countries in the world. To this day, Germans remain fascinated by this Cinderella story of a princess who was transformed into an empress not by some miracle, but by moving to Russia, an exotic country where anything is possible. For a while, German Chancellor Angela Merkel had a portrait of Catherine the Great on her desk. Obviously, Merkel, who, like the empress, was also from the territory of former East Germany, looked up to the tough Russian ruler who supposedly brought German order to Russia and went down in history as an exemplary absolute monarch.

The German fascination with Russia began during the reign of Catherine the Great. In 1763, the empress invited German colonists to Russia. To understand the context of this invitation, look no further than Friedrich Schiller's classic play *Intrigue and Love* (1784). In one of the scenes, which takes place at approximately the same time as Catherine's invitation, the duke sells off young men to serve as mercenaries in the American colonies in order to pay off his own debts. Most Germans were very poor in the second half of the 18th century, and emigration looked like winning the lottery, even if the conditions were tough. It's important to underscore the tens of thousands of Germans who accepted Catherine the Great's invitation to go to Russia received almost fairy tale-like resettlement conditions. The German colonists were guaranteed not only freedom of religion, but they were also released from military service, given money to start their new lives, awarded swaths of land, exempted from paying taxes for 30 years, and guaranteed local self-government. Such "benefits" are unimaginable, even in today's free economic zones. But in Catherine the Great's Russia, they were legendary.

One also must understand the conditions in which Russian peasants lived at the time.

E II

Catherine seized power following a coup and the murder of her husband Peter III. From the perspective of the Russian aristocracy, Catherine the Great wasn't a legitimate empress, which is why she started buying the nobility's loyalty by massively expanding their rights, particularly property rights over serfs. During her reign, serfs in the Russian Empire lost all their rights and became true slaves. The aristocrats could torture and kill serfs, rape women and children, and split up families (a husband, wife, and children could be sold to different owners in different regions of the country) with impunity. Therefore, compared with the status of Russian peasants, the lives of resettled German peasants seemed a dream come true.

Considerable differences between the Germans and the Russians could be seen in other segments of society as well. German architects were allowed to build in Russia what they couldn't back home, using disenfranchised serfs for labour. Almost every Russian writer or poet has a description of an ethnic German who cruelly oversees a strategic construction project or some other state or private enterprise. "It's over – the German is already laying the rails. The dead are buried in the ground; the sick hidden in trenches." This is how Russian poet Nikolai Nekrasov described the construction of the first Russian railway between Moscow and St. Petersburg in his poem "Railway" (1865). In another poem – "Who Lives Well in Russia" (1866) – he described a German estate supervisor, the aristocrat Vogel. A fictional but quite realistic character of the time, Vogel embodies all the negative traits of a German manager in Russia. He is exceedingly cruel, giving his subordinates harder and harder tasks. "The German has a deadly grip: he will suck until he leaves you a beggar," is what Russian peasants said about his management style. German supervisors of construction projects or aristocratic estates basically served as overseers of slaves, and were hired precisely for their cruelty and lack of emotional ties with their subordinates. This gave the Germans three privileges at once: being paid lots of money, receiving emotional satisfaction and feeling superior, and implementing projects which could not be realised back home.

The situation with the nobility was similar. The privileged German nobility – mainly from the Baltic Sea region – held a firm grip on power. According to Tomáš Masaryk's book *Russia and Europe* (1913), at the start of the 19th century, Germans were a disproportionately dominant group in the top political and military leadership of Russia. The Ministry of Internal Affairs was 27 per cent German, the military command 41 per cent, the Senate 33 per cent, the Ministry of Foreign Affairs 57 per cent, and the postal service 62 per cent German. Legend has it when Emperor Alexander I asked General Yermolov, whom he greatly admired, which award he wanted, the latter replied, "Make me a German," alluding to the privileged position of the Germans in the empire.

Of course, this seeming idyll was not perfect. The German diaspora in the Russian Empire also faced discrimination. The worst manifestation of anti-German sentiment in the empire was the series of pogroms in 1914 and 1915, when Russian mobs ransacked and robbed German businesses first in St. Petersburg and then in Moscow (a second and much larger wave of discrimination occurred in 1941, when Stalin's Soviet Union deported half a million Germans to Kazakhstan and other countries of Central Asia). They plundered the Emil Zindel textile factory, Einem confectionery factory, Ferrein pharmacy, and other German establishments. But despite this, for nearly two centuries, the Germans' attitude towards Russia was mostly optimistically positive.

The reason for this positive attitude is that, for 150 years, moving to Russia gave the Germans an opportunity to drastically change their lives, and receive the social, financial, and political capital to become the kind of people they were not back home: wealthy and influential members of the ruling class.

It would be naïve to say this attitude disappeared in the 20th century, when the countries fought against each other in two world wars, and then when the Soviet Union walled itself off from the West during the Cold War. National traditions remain traditions because they have a long history, and reappear at the first opportunity.

In 1964, a boy named Stefan was born to the Dürr family of farmers in Eberbach, in Germany's Baden-Württemberg region. He was interested in agriculture and enrolled in the agricultural science department of the University of Bayreuth – the Bavarian hometown of Wagner, known for its music festivals showcasing the composer's works. In 1989, as he proudly writes today on his company's website, Stefan was one of two West German students to participate in an internship exchange in the USSR at the state-owned collective pig farm named in honour of the "50th Anniversary of the USSR" in Naro-Fominsk, outside Moscow.

Today, it's hard to imagine what the collective farm would have looked like to the Bavarian student in the final years of the USSR, when even official Soviet publications were allowed to write about their filthy and poverty-stricken appearance, hopelessly abandoned by the staff. In contrast, it isn't hard to imagine what treatment the 23-year-old blond-haired Stefan from West Germany was given not only on the collective farm, but also in Moscow, which was just a few kilometres from Naro-Fominsk: he was given the imperial treatment of an esteemed colonial man among the natives.

Like the tens of thousands of Germans centuries before him, Stefan understood: in the destitute territories of central Russia, he could have what he couldn't back home – not only money, but respect and power. In 1991, he returned to intern in the USSR, this time at the collective farm named in honour of the "40th Anniversary of the October Revolution" near Kursk. And in 1993, he was appointed an advisor to the Russian State *Duma* on agricultural reform and the German-Russian agrarian policy dialogue.

As a student in Germany, Stefan was guaranteed stable but not exceptional prospects of working in an industry primarily relying on subsidies. Farmers' voices aren't often influential in the European Union because they are spread out among all the countries pursuing their own national interests. Being a successful farmer in Bavaria or Württemberg meant your influence was limited to that region and extended at most to city hall. It's an honest but provincial life. Russia offered Stefan a whole new calibre of influence.

In 1994, Stefan started the agricultural company EkoNiva. In 1998, he began importing Western agricultural machinery and seeds into Russia. In 2002, he established subsidiaries in the Russian regions. In 2006, Dürr built livestock breeding complexes for 1,400 cows, and the following year won Russian prizes and the Order of Merit of the Federal Republic of Germany. Stefan was visited by governors and even by the president of Russia – to honour a "proper German" who "understands the deep connection" between Germany and Russia. In 2013, Russian President Vladimir Putin granted Dürr Russian citizenship. By the way, giving Russian citizenship to German entrepreneurs is a fairly common practice by the Russian government. For example, in 2016, after Russia had already attacked Ukraine, Andrea von Knoop, the long-time president of the German-Russian Chamber of Commerce and member of the German-Russian Forum Board in Berlin, was granted Russian citizenship. Nevertheless, Stefan Dürr was quick to act on the opportunities Russian citizenship offers.

In 2014, Russia attacked Ukraine and it was Stefan Dürr who approached President Putin with the idea of declaring sanctions against the West and banning the import of agricultural products into Russia. Putin listened to the good German and in 2014 Dürr's company EkoNiva became the largest milk producer in Russia.

The thirst for glory or power, money, or one's mystical personal desires – which of these prevailed in the story of the West German student who followed the example of an 18th-century settler and was transformed into a courtier? In 2012, the German magazine *Der Spiegel* published an article about Dürr. "When he enters a kindergarten, it looks like an impromptu state visit. Tea is suddenly served. A guest book is pulled out. The children line up to take a picture with the *latifundista* (landowner) and give him hand-crafted gifts." In 2017, the Franco-German TV channel *Arte* produced a documentary about Dürr. In it, Dürr proudly says he built a church in the village where his company's headquarters is located. "I needed a church. Building a church was my passion," Dürr claims in the film. "The village head wasn't happy. He said: if you have the money, then build a hospital." Dürr built a church anyway.

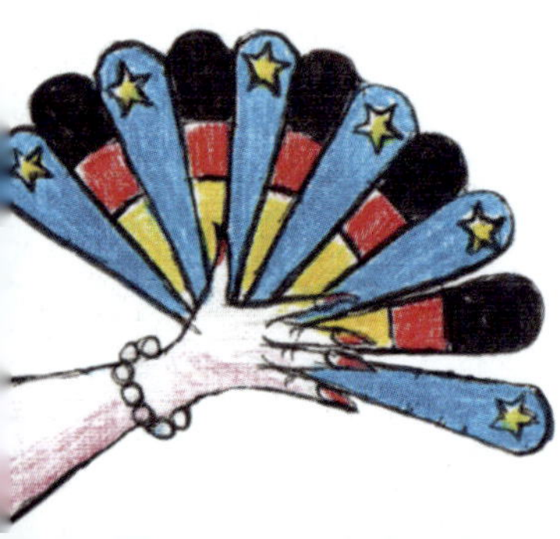

But it would be a mistake to say the German fascination with Russia is based solely on money and advancing careers. Yes, making lots of money and becoming a local quasi-prince and advisor to the president of a nuclear state is a powerful incentive. But something else was needed for financial interest to turn into true love: German mysticism, which was and remains part of the German national worldview. Like the financial and career-based fondness for Russia, this motivation has a long history.

Boundless Dominance

In 1900, one of the greatest German authors, Rainer Maria Rilke, wrote the story "How Treason Came to Russia." It begins with a conversation between two neighbours. The narrator has just returned from a trip. He meets his neighbour, Ewald, a lame man who looks out his window attentively every day.

"Good morning, Ewald," I stepped up to his window as I always did in passing. "I was away."

"Where have you been?" he asked impatiently.

"In Russia."

"Oh, so far away," he leaned back, and continued: "What kind of a country is it, Russia? Very large, isn't it?"

"Yes," I said, "it is large, but besides for that..."

"Did I ask a stupid question?" smiled Ewald, blushing.

"No, Ewald, on the contrary. You're asking what kind of country it is makes various things clearer for me. For instance, what countries border Russia."

"On the east?" my friend interrupted.

I paused for a moment to reflect.

"No."

"On the north?" inquired the lame man.

"You see," I had an inspiration, "maps have spoiled people. There, everything is flat and even, and when the four points of the compass are indicated on the map, they think that's all there is to know. But a country is not a map. It has mountains and valleys. It must border something both above and below."

"Hm," my friend considered. "You are right. But what could Russia border on in those two directions?" His facial expression transformed into one of an innocent child.

"You know..." I encouraged him to figure it out.

"Perhaps on God?"

"Yes," I confirmed, "on God."

This one moment of enlightenment can be dissected into dozens of layers. As so happens when something is written by a true genius, Rilke wonderfully mirrored Vladimir Putin's conversation with a schoolboy in front of the TV cameras in November 2016, during an awards ceremony for students by the Russian Geographical Society. Putin asked one of the schoolchildren where Russia's borders end. "At the Bering Strait, with the USA on the opposite shore," Miroslav Oskirko began his answer. The Russian dictator interrupted the boy and said, "Russia's borders don't end anywhere."

In Rilke's story, Russia's lack of borders turned it into a spiritual empire where the tsar was God's deputy. Which is why the Russians loved and feared the tsar: all the greatest powers were combined in him. Although the German author was writing about Ivan the Terrible, undoubtedly, he was referring to any leader of Russia. And these views were shared by more than Rilke's character. The view that in Russia unlimited tyranny is a natural state, one Western observers can only but admire and exoticize, exists to this day. The idea dictator Vladimir Putin is the most natural leader for Russia because the people want a strong ruler, could be heard for years from Germans working with Russia. You would often also hear them make comments about Russia's absence of borders.

"Russia is our neighbour," (and this is why you must negotiate with Russia, while ignoring the interests of the countries of Central and Eastern Europe) is a standard phrase used in every German political debate in recent decades. It was spoken by nearly every German politician, including those most critical of the Kremlin (but still in love with Russia). The idea, "Russia is our neighbour," has become so mainstream, it raises the question: where did it come from? Is Russia really a neighbour of Germany? Of course not. Germany's neighbours to the east are Poland and Czechia, if you don't count the Kaliningrad Oblast (former East Prussia), which, until the 1960s, was drawn on German maps as part of West Germany when giving the weather forecast for Königsberg or registering automobile license plates. Poland's and Czechia's eastern neighbours are Lithuania, Belarus, Ukraine, and Slovakia. And Russia, which has a border with Ukraine, is a third order neighbour. But as Rilke's character said, don't look at maps, they'll only spoil the mystical sense of a "great Russia."

The perception of a Russia with no borders, slumbering in the snow, wielding unlimited power and resources, possessed of a mysterious spirituality, ready to live without the comforts of modern society in its own unique way, always seeking a true tsar, etc., etc., etc., fascinated and continues to fascinate Germans. Today, it's difficult to say whether Russian poet Fyodor Tyutchev came up with the quote Russia "cannot be understood with the mind alone," you can "only believe in it" on his own, or whether he, as a Russian diplomat in the Kingdom of

Bavaria, heard it from a German. Although there is a third possibility: this phrase could have been part of Tyutchev's mission from Emperor Nicholas I to create a positive attitude towards Russia in Europe. Whichever of these three versions is correct, the attitude towards Russia being a state and society which cannot be judged by common measures (therefore, they can be forgiven almost everything, because they are unique and incapable of normal behaviour) prevails in Germany to this day.

In fact, for decades Germany has been creating its own, singular image of Russia. From the point of view of modern political ethics, it could be interpreted as a racist view or appropriation (in some ways it is). Germany created images for domestic consumption embodying everything incomprehensible, wild, and fascinating German society admired, projecting them onto an imaginary, fictitious Russia.

This fiction about Russia, and infatuation with it, was present in every iteration of German statehood. There was space for this infatuation even when German chauvinism reached its peak under the Nazis. In 1939–1940, the acclaimed Austrian film director Gustav Ucicky made a film *Der Postmeister (The Postmaster)* based on Alexander Pushkin's book *The Stationmaster* (1831). The leading role in the film was played by renown German actor Heinrich George, who also starred in the masterpiece *Metropolis* (1927). The film, where the officers' fur hats are set against endless snowy fields, and extravagant champagne parties lead to absurd love scenes with incredibly beautiful Russian women, reflected all the clichés about Russia. This love for Russia existed outside Germany as well. In 1940, the film won the Mussolini Cup for best foreign film at the Venice Film Festival. Interestingly, Ucicky was directing another film at the same time as he was making his panegyric on Russia: *Homecoming*, a Nazi anti-Polish propaganda film depicting the alleged relentless oppression by the Poles of the German minority in Lutsk. Also interesting is the fact the film's star, Heinrich George, was arrested in 1945 by the Soviet security services and sent to the concentration camp in Sachsenhausen, then already under the control of the USSR, and was murdered by starvation while imprisoned by the Soviet occupying forces.

The romanticisation of Russia in *The Postmaster* was no longer appropriate after the Nazis attacked their former Soviet allies in June 1941, and the film was banned. But a few years later, after the Nazi Reich fell, the love for fur and snow returned to its former state of affairs.

A fat, stocky man with an unruly bushy beard, wearing a tall fur hat shaped like a house, dressed in red velvet garments trimmed with gold and fur, and with garish rings on his fingers, walks onto the stage. It's the 1960s and the singer is Ivan Rebroff – the face of traditional Russian music, the "golden voice" of Germany, star of numerous albums and performer of Russian-language songs which made German hearts melt. Rebroff was born Hans-Rolf Rippert in Berlin in 1931. He began to perform, including singing Russian songs, and at one point his mentor suggested he sing exclusively in Russian. And thus, the German singer Ivan Rebroff "was born" and went on to make millions. He was an ambassador of Russian culture in Germany until his death in 2008.

Rebroff was just one of many examples of how Russian musical culture was exoticized. The existence of countless "Don Cossack" choirs and other musical performers who are famous only in Germany – not in Russia – support this phenomenon. The image of Russia is, on one hand, that of a country with remarkable opportunities, and, on the other hand, a mystical territory of endless snow, unusual music, golden-domed churches, and frightening, but very attractive, authoritarianism.

Notably, the love of Russian authoritarianism and readiness to forgive Russia for any international crimes it commits is often seen in parallel with German anti-Americanism. This is odd, since it was

the United States which freed Germany from the totalitarian Nazi regime and did not impose another form of totalitarianism on the Germans, like Moscow did. Cooperation with the US helped the West Germans build up their economy, achieve the highest quality of life in German history, and for the first time in history build a stable German democracy. It was the presence of the US in Europe that protected West Germany from a Soviet invasion and saved West Berlin during the Soviet blockade in 1947–1948. Meanwhile, the Soviet occupation of East Germany brought with it a totalitarian dictatorship, arrests of innocent people, the construction of a closed society, and ultimately led East Germany to economic collapse. Nevertheless, in the minds of many Germans, Russia looks like a reliable partner and important pillar of world democracy, while the United States undermines international stability. According to a survey of Germans in 2019 by the Centre for Strategy and Higher Leadership in Cologne, 59 per cent of respondents considered the US the biggest threat to world peace. The second biggest threat, according to the Germans, was North Korea, followed by Turkey and Russia; 21 per cent of eastern Germans polled considered Russia a threat, compared to 45 per cent of western Germans.

What's the secret behind this anti-Americanism and love of Russia? Certainly, there are many explanations. Some believe the Germans consider the US part of the Western world, and therefore demand more from it than Russia, which by default is perceived as "foreign" and "different." But it seems the real answer lies elsewhere. On some level, most Germans understand the US will always be the cultural, technological, economic, and military leader in the trans-Atlantic partnership. Germany remains a subordinate, a weaker partner, despite the Germans' certainty of their cultural and technological superiority.

Meanwhile, in contrast with being the weaker partner to America, a partnership with Russia promises Germany completely different prospects. In an alliance with Moscow, Berlin would play first fiddle on economic and technology issues, leaving military matters and world politics to the Russians. Moreover, by siding with Russia, those German elites who dislike the overly egalitarian nature of the US and Western democracy in general, can finally move to a more anti-egalitarian, hierarchical, racist, misogynistic, and conservative way of life. In this union, you can ignore the interests of Poland and Ukraine, women and minorities, even your own downtrodden social groups, while restoring the traditions of Prussia and other monarchical and conservative (and stuck in the 19th century) German states. Leaping into the arms of Moscow becomes an act of revenge against the US, revenge for building an overly free, open, globalist, and technological society in Germany. Unlike the German dream of a conservative, somewhat backwards and anti-progressive society (a society where doctors prescribe and insurance companies cover homeopathy, where communication with state authorities is (still) done via fax, and which has one of the world's strictest bans on Google Maps photographing streets), which shuts itself in, and in every discussion – sooner or later – starts scolding the US for having once attacked Iraq.

So, Russian authoritarianism isn't something scaring off many Germans. It is more likely the contrary; it may attract more interest towards Russia. But like other factors in German-Russian relations, this phenomenon should also be explored in terms of economics, not just morality. For many years, some of the most active pro-Russian lobbyists were German businesses operating in Russia. Germany's economic interest in Russia was unusual. In the media and politics, Russia was portrayed as one of Germany's most important economic partners, a partner who can and must be forgiven any transgressions because of this importance. But Russia's importance has always been a myth without a foundation in reality.

For example, in 2021, the volume of trade between Germany and Russia was €59.8 billion. That same year, the volume of trade between Germany and Poland was €146.8 billion, nearly three times more in absolute terms, or 9.3 times more per capita. This fact, however, didn't make Poland an "important eastern partner and neighbour" the same way the business and political community painted Russia.

What's more, in 2021 Germany's total volume of foreign trade globally was €2.579 trillion (€1.2 trillion in imports and €1.3 trillion in exports). Thus, Russia accounted for only 2.3 per cent of German foreign trade. This figure, of course, is more than what could be seen as within the statistical margin of error, but it's not something extraordinary. For example, in terms of German exports, Russia as a buyer country ranks 14th, between Hungary and Sweden. When it comes to countries selling goods to Germany, Russia was in 12th place, after Spain and before the United Kingdom.

Obviously, the image of Russia as an extremely important partner has been based on something more than economic statistics. Of course, much of Russia's economic influence is rooted in Germany's dependence on Russian gas. During the construction of the first (still Soviet) gas pipelines to Germany, the West German political elites adopted an unofficial rule: Germany's dependence on a single gas supplier cannot exceed 20 per cent of the country's overall gas needs. After former German Chancellor Gerhard Schröder went to work in the Russian energy sector and under Chancellor Angela Merkel, this dependence jumped to more than 40 per cent. Russian gas wasn't only used for energy: many chemical companies depended on Russian raw materials. Given the structure of German exports is similar to newly industrialised countries (the export of goods far exceeds the export of services), it's hard to overestimate the importance of cheap raw materials. Thanks to the titanic efforts of "Green" economy minister Robert Habeck, Germany managed to give up Russian gas in the second half of 2022. But for 50 years, German industry lived and thrived under circumstances where gas contracts with Russia were the norm.

Additionally, the Russian market, although not vital for the economy overall, is key for certain companies and industries. For example, at the start of Russia's war against Ukraine in 2014, Russia was the fifth largest market for German machine manufacturers, after China, the US, France, and the United Kingdom. For some companies, mainly from former East Germany, Russia is their first or second largest market.

The Russian World of German Privilege

But the main lobbyists for special relations with Russia aren't even companies – they're the German managers working in Russia. For years, the German community in Moscow wilfully turned itself into a powerful pro-Russian lobby. And we're not talking about businessmen like Stefan Dürr. At the start of the war in 2014, some 6,000 German companies were working in Russia (and almost none of them left after the annexation of Ukraine's Crimean Peninsula). Most of these companies had German management, at least on the level of the general director of the rep office. What does a move to Moscow mean for the manager of a medium-sized German company? The same thing it meant in the 18th century for a poor German craftsman or an impoverished aristocrat who moved to St. Petersburg: a significant increase in social capital and living standards.

No relocation within the EU offers a German manager such an increase in influence and income as a move to Moscow. First of all, the salary in Russia is typically higher, to compensate for the distance from home, climate, and other difficult working conditions. Secondly, thanks to the Russian-German agreement on the avoidance of double taxation, they only pay a 13 per cent income tax on their salary. And to be even more attractive to Western expats, Russia allows Western managers to get special work visas which don't require them to pay any social security payments from their salary other than this minimal tax. Compared with German taxes and social security contributions, this looks like a ticket to a neoliberal paradise.

There are other bonuses to working in Moscow. Managers who did not have a company car at home often get one in Moscow, if for no other reason than the legendary Moscow traffic jams. For security reasons and to boost the company's image, they live in fancy apartments in the city centre, often nicer than their homes in Germany. Their lifestyle is more like one of a colonial officer than a German manager in Dusseldorf or Hamburg. Inappropriate treatment of subordinate local staff, especially women, which would normally have very negative consequences back home, is tolerated in Moscow. Respect for the labour code or adherence to (practically non-existent) anti-discrimination legislation depends mostly on the good graces of the managers. Subordinates can be fired at will and forced to work overtime without compensation, and, of course, women can be harassed and sexualised, justifying this as "a Russian tradition" the German management supposedly respects and follows to a tee.

Working in Russia also allows you to enjoy other, usually forbidden, aspects of life. For example, Matthias Schepp, who for many years was the Moscow bureau chief for *Der Spiegel* magazine, wrote in his 2009 book *Instruction for Moscow* how his kids once demanded in Germany he "drive the way he did in Moscow," and couldn't understand why their dad didn't do so. After working as a journalist in Moscow for many years, Schepp, who has a Russian wife and owns a home in Russia, became chairman of the German-Russian Chamber of Commerce in 2016.

Every aspect of the daily work of a German manager in Russia smacks of seduction. In Germany, the construction of large infrastructure projects requires many years of negotiations and compromises with local authorities, environmental and cultural associations, and even private homeowners. But in Russia, large projects can be started on the basis of a political decision. And not just projects like the Olympic Village in Sochi, where hundreds of homes were razed, and local residents were forcibly resettled to make way for hotels and other buildings constructed using German suppliers. Any German company making the decision to "localise" production (ie, move production to Russia), is given a green light from political sponsors. A German plant could get land without a problem, and, if the decision was made on the level of the president or Cabinet of Ministers, they knew the local authorities would not risk arguing with a politically backed project. Nowhere in Europe can a manager enjoy the luxury of driving the course of history, conquering nature, and building mega-projects – only in Russia. For German managers, this is one of only a few opportunities to take on the role of a colonial officer building a railroad somewhere in the German colony of Namibia in the 19th century: ignoring the locals, laying new routes, conquering nature.

In general, Moscow offers an opportunity to enjoy life without worrying too much about morality or empathy. The quality of service in Moscow for the top strata of customers is very different than in Germany. Almost all managers list the same perks in Moscow: 24-hour luxury goods stores, the ability to order any service at any time, relatively cheap luxury taxis, digitalisation of services, including online payments, high interest rates on bank deposits, convenient airports with 24-hour flights (most German airports have night flight bans or restrictions in the interest of residents of nearby cities). It's hard to say whether the policy of the government-owned airline Aeroflot regarding foreign business customers was approved on the political level, but the fact remains: getting an Aeroflot Bonus Gold Card with frequent upgrades to business class is incomparably easier than with European airlines: take 50 flights in any class and at any price in a calendar year. Moreover, the flight attendants on Aeroflot flights to Europe look like models. Official internal management documents at Aeroflot reveal women over the age of 40 or with a clothing size over 48 were taken off flights to Europe and reassigned to domestic flights. A German manager with an economy class ticket from Frankfurt to Moscow and a Gold Card had an excellent chance of being upgraded to business class, where he would be welcomed with warm nuts and a glass of sparkling wine served by a flight attendant in a tight orange skirt and heavy makeup, crouching in front of him and saying with a smile: "My name is Irina. What is your name?" It is a non-stop ticket to a completely different life.

In some way, European sanctions even played into the hands of those German managers who remained in Russia. It was extremely important for the Kremlin to show "ordinary people" and "ordinary businesses" do not support the restrictions of the West. That's why Kremlin working groups tasked with attracting German businessmen and managers received maximum attention after the annexation of Ukraine's Crimean Peninsula. Never was the topic of a "single trading space from Lisbon to Vladivostok" more popular than after 2015. Small and medium-sized German businesses remaining in Moscow gained an incredible opportunity to regularly attend working breakfasts at the Russian Foreign Ministry and a level of attention from the national authorities they never would have had back home. Russia has always known how to buy people through their vanity. It gave German business the opportunity to feel more influential, more important, and smarter than it really is.

The extent to which this moral poison dulled reality can be seen in a survey of German businesses released in December 2021 by the German-Russian Chamber of Commerce. According to the study, 48 per cent of German companies working in Russia believed German-Russian business relations were good or very good. Moreover, 62 per cent expected economic growth in 2022. As for the Nord Stream 2 pipeline, 44 per cent of businessmen believed it should be put into operation, even with the missing technical permits. Only 22 per cent of those surveyed believed safeguards should be put in place to avoid Russia potentially using the gas pipeline to exert political pressure. In other words, German businessmen who were working in Russia, who should have been most cognisant of Russia and its behaviour, whose salary depended precisely on being experts in understanding Russia, not only did not foresee Russia would start a European war two months later, but also couldn't even imagine the country would resort to gas blackmail.

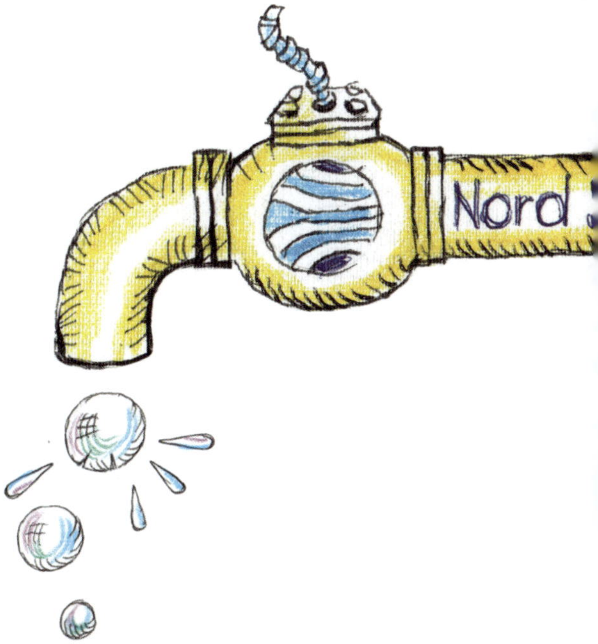

This dependence on toxic Russian resources – not gas, but power, influence, and dirty money – worked in an interesting way in favour of the German authorities. Starting in the mid-2000s, Russian companies, mostly with state or semi-state capital, started hunting for weak German assets. In 2008, the Russian state-owned Sberbank initiated the process of acquiring the German automobile manufacturer Opel. The German company was a wholly owned subsidiary of the American company General Motors, which was hit hard by the global economic crisis. According to GM's internal policy, Opels were only sold in Europe, and there was only a minimal demand for them. During the global economic crisis, budget car buyers weren't looking to buy new cars. Opel faced bankruptcy, and the company's tens of thousands of employees faced losing their jobs.

Russia's Sberbank had zero experience investing in automobile production, but its CEO Herman Gref – the Kremlin's man – wanted to enter the German market and increase Sberbank's presence in the European market after having acquired a Czech bank and rebranded it as Sberbank CZ. Sberbank's proposal was transparent: the Russians buy a nearly bankrupt German company, introduce the brand to the Russian market, and guarantee jobs. In autumn 2009, Herman Gref visited the Frankfurt Auto Show and sat in a position of honour during the Opel presentation. The Germans obviously considered him the new owner of the German company. But the US government's unexpected bailout of the American automotive industry put a stop to the purchase, and the Russians were forced to go home without Opel. Their desire to gain influence in Rüsselsheim, the city in the state of Hessen where Opel directly employed 20,000 people and indirectly provided jobs for tens of thousands more there as well as in other German communities, was not realised. But this didn't mean the Russians didn't put their concept into practice in other German cities and regions.

In the 2000s, the Russians made a number of investments which strengthened their strategic influence in Germany. Rosneft under the management of Putin's pal Igor Sechin purchased German oil plants, and German gas storage facilities were acquired by Russia's Gazprom. These investments were obviously made to have political leverage over Germany. Other Russian investments, however, are far more cunning.

In 2008, in the north German state of Mecklenburg-Western Pomerania, Wadan Yards began having significant financial problems. The company, which made ferries and freight vessels, couldn't compete with South Korean ship building companies and was headed towards bankruptcy. Founded in 1946 in East Germany, it couldn't handle global competition: its ships were too expensive, and the financial transactions took too long. Strategically, this meant Wismar – an old Hanseatic city with a population of 40,000 – would lose at least 1,500 jobs and thousands of other jobs relying on the shipyards would be at risk. The city faced a potential economic disaster.

In 2008, the Minister President of Mecklenburg-Western Pomerania started a campaign to save Wadan. During a meeting with Russian President Dmitry Medvedev, he lobbied the Russians to purchase the shipyards. He didn't have to wait long. In June 2009, the nearly bankrupt shipyards were bought by the young, 30-year-old investor Vitaly Yusufov – the millionaire son of former Russian energy minister and Gazprom board member Igor Yusufov, who was close to then Russian President Dmitry Medvedev. The leadership of the German state was overjoyed the company was rescued, and the Russian investors were happy to get a good deal on a vital enterprise in an important city in the region, making them key players in German regional politics.

To reinforce their success, the Russians made another investment: another company close to Dmitry Medvedev – Ilim Timber – purchased the wood processing plant that was one of the largest partners of the Wismar port. Investors close to Medvedev essentially made the Mecklenburg–Western Pomerania region dependent on their good will. If the Russian investors left, it's unlikely the local authorities would have found new buyers. Simply put, the first hint of a threat of the Russians leaving the market made the local authorities compliant. In Germany, regional governments have a great deal of influence on federal policy. Formally, regional representatives can block any law with their votes in the *Bundesrat;* and informally, regional governments take part in all political debates in the country.

The increase in Russian influence in Mecklenburg–Western Pomerania wasn't accidental; this is where the Russian Nord Stream 2 gas pipeline reaches German territory. It was the state government of Mecklenburg–Western Pomerania which founded the Climate and Environment Protection Foundation MV which received money from Gazprom and invested its own capital to purchase equipment for the gas pipelines. Minister President Sellering, the very same one who invited Dmitry Medvedev to invest in regional companies, was the chairman of the foundation. Were these the only Russian investments in the region? No. In 2016, the Russian Kirov Plant invested in the production of bearings in Rostock, another city in the state. The opening of the plant, with 50 (!) employees and a capacity to produce 200 bearings annually, was attended by Russian Minister

of Industry and Energy Denis Manturov. Interestingly, back in 2013, the Kirov Plant made its first attempt to enter Germany via the traditional scheme of buying bankrupt companies: the Russians bought the Göppel Bus manufacturer, whose business was in a slump, and before that, the tools manufacturer Monforts Werkzeugmaschinen, which was teetering on the brink of bankruptcy.

Russian economic influence in Germany is built around a simple principle: Russia gives ineffective German businesses and the overall ineffective German economic model new life. For years, Germany's export-oriented producers bought cheap Russian gas, and paid for it with European security. German regions selfishly rescued their bankrupt local manufacturers by giving the Russians leverage over their politicians. German companies operating in Russia became hostages of their managers, who were interested in the quality of their own private lives and having the privileges of white colonial masters. German politicians satisfied their anti-American obsessions through their sense of closeness to the legendary sources of power and resources in Moscow.

Germany's dependence on Russia doesn't go back decades, it goes back centuries, and is built on toxic narratives of power, violence, and deception. It was and remains anti-European and intent on being in conflict with the ideals of freedom, equality, and openness. It has no objective basis other than the radically nationalist and cultish-mystical myth of Russia's "special spiritual idea" and Germany's "closeness" to this idea. And that is why Germany's "special relationship" with Russia is a threat to Europe and to world peace.

Nord Stre

The Epistle of Baltic Hippies

Story by Oleksii Dubrov
Illustrated by Andrii Yermolenko

IT WAS UNEXPECTEDLY SUNNY and warm for Kaunas in May 1972. The city, once the capital of the Lithuanian Republic, had not suffered much damage during WWII, unlike many other European cities such as Rotterdam and Warsaw. The city centre had been preserved, and attracted tourists from all over the USSR, hoping to catch a glimpse of "Europe" and breathe the air of relative freedom.

The city's main street – *Laisves Aleya* or Liberty Avenue – was distinctive in its charm and serenity. Two parallel lanes divided by rows of ancient linden trees, precisely placed benches, and flowerbeds extended through the main stretch of the avenue, which in total ran for 1.6km. The street had retained its original name, despite predictions it would be renamed "Lenin" or "Soviet" Avenue. In 1972, cars still drove on the street, passing by modern facades, and those of two- and three-story pre-revolutionary buildings with little regard. After the war, the "competent" city managers commissioned several new Soviet structures, whose drab appearance stuck out amid the style of the 600-year-old historical city centre.

The right side of the avenue, bedecked in green and red tulips freshly planted for the upcoming May Day celebrations, was overcome with the aroma of freshly baked bread from the *Konditerija* or Confectionary. This pleasing scent, while laced with exhaust fumes from brand-new *Zhyhuli* cars, was nevertheless tempting to hungry engineering and economics students who waited in line on their breaks from the nearby Kaunas Polytechnical University. The Soviet Union occupied a sixth of the world's land mass, and yet Kaunas drew visitors from across the country, for work, to serve in the army, or to visit friends. Visitors were mesmerised by signage featuring the Latin alphabet and deceived themselves into thinking they had crossed the border. The Baltic people (or the Pre-Baltic as they were known back then) were considered "different" than the rest of the Soviets; although they had been forced to join the Soviet Union in 1940, their behaviour was distinct from others in the USSR. In the 1970s, women freely wore trousers here, as opposed to cities such as Kyiv, where women adhered to Soviet fashions of the time. For many, these Pre-Baltic individuals were considered as some sort of "Soviet Germans."

The hippie movement was also a notable peculiarity here, characterised by young people in torn jeans and loose shirts, with long hair, playing guitars. They often gathered around the fountain in Minsk Park near the Musical Theatre and played Luxembourg Rock Radio on their portable tape recorders and radios. The rock station was banned by the government, but the music became an expression of the yearning for freedom. Occasionally, the *militsiya* (militarised police) or special detachments of the All-Union Leninist Young Communist League (also known as the *Komsomol*) would come around, beat up the hippies, and chase them away, making a show of cutting their hair. Some members of the group were arrested and imprisoned for up to 15 days under the charge of "petty hooliganism." In 1971, these groups protested in Grodno (Belarus), Vilnius, and Moscow with slogans like "Hands off long hair!", "Freedom for rock-n-roll!", "Stop the militsiya terror tactics!" and "All you need is love." Ukrainian hippies from Lviv actively participated in the protests. Meanwhile, the rest of the city continued, on the whole, to lead a routine Brezhnevite existence.

Then, on Sunday, 14 May 1972, clouds darkened the sky. The Kaunas hippies had planned a get-together to put on an underground performance of the musical *Hair*. At 12.30pm that day, everything changed. A young man with long hair, a moustache and a beard walked up to the fountain. He pulled a three-litre gas can out of his woven mesh bag, poured the contents of the can over himself, and shouted out "Freedom for Lithuania!" before lighting himself on fire. A potent smell of seared flesh tinged with gasoline permeated the park and surrounding area. Onlookers rushed to the scene, attempting to douse the flames, but the gas had done its job. Nearby, they found a note declaring "The *system* is responsible for my death."

The 19-year-old died the next day in the hospital from extensive burns. His name was Romas Kalanta.

Romas Kalanta was born in the city of Alytus in southern Lithuania in February 1953, a few days before Stalin died. His father was a veteran of the most recent war with the Germans and a member of the Communist Party of the Soviet Union (CPSU). His mother worked in retail. When Romas was 10 years old his family moved to Kaunas where his father was offered a position as a lecturer at the Polytechnical Institute. The boy was enrolled in School #18. There is evidence every year the family secretly celebrated Lithuanian Independence Day on 16 February. This didn't seem to interfere with his father's willingness to cooperate with the occupation government, working as their lackey, or as it is described in Western literature, a "fellow traveller."

Romas was kicked out of the Komsomol in high school after vocalising anti-government views during a meeting of the History Club. At age 17, he became eager to get his high school diploma so he could attend the seminary (his mother was a devout Catholic). However, he was unable to pass the final exams, so he took a job and attended night school, planning to complete his studies the following year. Several of his friends were part of the hippie movement, refusing to live the lives of "typical Soviet citizens." Romas was a poet, played guitar, participated in sports, and occasionally met up with his hippie friends at Minsk Park where they often gathered. Communists did not approve of people like Romas, their distrust based on the words of Lenin, who believed "One cannot live in society and be free from society." Romas realised the only way to take control of his life was to die by suicide, determining his own fate through this act of protest.

Kaunas exploded.

On 18 and 19 May, four days after Kalanta's death, 3,000 schoolchildren and young people protested on Liberty Avenue. They chanted anti-Soviet slogans: "Freedom for Lithuania!" and "Russians go home!" The occupation administration arrested more than 400 protesters, eight of whom were sentenced to several years in prison for the aforementioned "hooliganism." But this did not stop the Lithuanians from further acts of protest; in 1972 alone, according to official documents, 13 people followed in the footsteps of Romas Kalanta and self-immolated. The events of May 1972 went down in history as the "Kaunas Spring," and the city itself was known for some time as *Kalantagrad*. The hippie movement, already despised by the regime, was repressed by the KGB, despite the fact Romas was never an official member. The agency never wasted such an opportunity to rid itself of a problem.

Nevertheless, no matter how hard the communists tried to conceal Kalanta's act of protest, the news spread throughout the Lithuanian diaspora, who began to speak about it widely. The Lithuanian writer Alantas Vitautas, who was living in the US at the time, wrote an academic study in 1976 on Romas Kalanta, and later published three poems about him. Lithuanians became increasingly aware of Romas and his act of protest while listening to foreign radio broadcasts. Even without the Internet, news spread far.

Self-immolation is a desperate act, one used when all other forms of protest have been exhausted, or there is simply no other way to bring attention to a problem. The first notable act of self-immolation was the suicide of the Buddhist monk Thich Quang Duc in Saigon (then South Vietnam) on 11 June 1963. He was protesting the persecution of Buddhists by the South Vietnamese President Ngo Dinh Diem, who was Catholic. By the next morning, a photograph of the act had circled the globe, and American President John Kennedy commented that, *"No news picture in history has generated so much emotion around the world as that one."* The monk's suicide sparked protests, and President Ngo Dinh Diem was assassinated several months later in reaction. The photographer Malcolm Browne won the Pulitzer Prize for his photo of Thich Quang Duc during the self-immolation.

Interestingly, even the Chinese media published the photo of Thich Quang Duc, while the major Soviet newspapers *Pravda* and *Izvestia* completely ignored the event. It may have been because of the religious motivation for the self-immolation, or more likely, because at the time, the first female Soviet astronaut, Valentina Tereshkova, currently a member of the Russian *Duma* and rabid supporter of Putin and his invasion of Ukraine, was about to travel to space. Her flight and the great victory for "Soviet women and the Party" dominated the headlines for a week. Even when the South Vietnamese president was assassinated in November 1963, there was no mention of the Buddhist monk; the Soviet government did not want to see a repetition of the monk's protest in the USSR. But when a totalitarian regime prohibits all other means of protest, it cannot be avoided. The self-immolation of Jan Palach, a student in Prague in 1969, became the symbol of the struggle against the Soviet occupation of Central and Eastern Europe. His act was in protest of the use of force deployed to crush the "Prague Spring," and his funeral turned into a widespread political demonstration.

These kinds of protests were not uncommon in Ukraine either. In 1968, a veteran of *UPA* (the Ukrainian Insurgent Army) Vasyl Makukh cried out "Occupiers, get out!" and "Long live a free Ukraine!", drenched himself with three litres of gasoline, and set himself on fire. The event took place on Khreshchatyk Street in the centre of the capital Kyiv on 5 November, just before the annual celebration of the anniversary of the "October Revolution." The militsiya quickly cordoned off the area of protest, to prevent anyone from seeing what had occurred.

On 21 January 1978, at around 3.00am, one day before the 60th anniversary of the declaration of independence of the Ukrainian National Republic, the dissident Oleksa Hirnyk self-immolated on the deserted *Chernecha Hora*, or Taras Hill, in Kaniv. He had scattered around a thousand anti-Soviet flyers on the hill before he died, and the next morning most of these flyers were gathered up by the militsiya. The KGB went to great lengths to keep his protest quiet.

In October 2020, Mykola Mykytenko, a veteran of the Russian-Ukrainian War, lit himself on fire on Khreshchatyk Street to protest the withdrawal of troops from the line of contact, which had resulted in the strengthening of the Russian occupation of Ukraine's Donbas. Sadly, even today, there are instances when the government and society stubbornly refuse to listen to their citizens. Neither the incident with Mykytenko, nor those of Makukh and Hirnyk, led to protests or resonated at all in Ukrainian society, as similar acts did for the Vietnamese, the Czechs, and the Lithuanians.

Romas Kalanta never lived in a free Lithuania. The Soviet Union sought to occupy the country for 20 years after the fall of the Russian Tsarist Empire. They only succeeded in 1940, and the majority of Kalanta's older peers remembered this. The same happened with Lithuania's neighbours Latvia and Estonia. After the Soviet army invaded, thousands of their citizens emigrated to the West, and established formidable Baltic diaspora communities. They never accepted the occupation and maintained contact with their families in their homeland. It was thanks to the diaspora that the residents of the republics wore jeans and listened to forbidden Western music.

The Baltic diaspora regularly raised the question of independence with Western elites. As a result of their activism, the United States and the NATO member states never recognised the occupation of the Baltic countries. In 1960 and 1983, resolutions were adopted condemning the annexation of the Baltic states and keeping the Baltic question on the world's daily agenda, if only theoretically.

At the end of the 1980s, the Soviet Union was living out its last years. Ever more frequently, the secret pact between the USSR and Nazi Germany, the so-called Molotov-Ribbentrop Pact signed in 1939, was being discussed publicly. According to its Secret Protocol, Lithuania, Latvia, and Estonia were awarded to Stalin. The Baltic population realised they were not simply treacherously occupied, but they had been pawns in the cynical bartering between two totalitarian regimes. They had been treated like slaves. The anger that had been silenced for decades roared onto the streets. On 23 August 1987, the anniversary of the signing of the Pact, the first protests broke out. Exactly one year later, the anti-Soviet demonstration in Vilnius was attended by 250,000 protesters. In 1989, a massive undertaking named the Baltic Way united the three countries with a 600km-long human chain. Several months later, Ukrainians followed the Baltic countries' lead, forming a human chain uniting all of Ukraine.

From the first moments of their renewed independence, the Baltic countries had a clear goal in mind: to return to Europe.

In the spring of 1990, Lithuania and Latvia made the decision to "re-establish independence." Their choice of words played a decisive role; though 50 years had passed, the people had not forgotten their enemy and occupier. Moreover, those who were born and lived in independent Latvian and Lithuanian states were still alive.

"The Supreme Council of the Republic of Lithuania, *expressing the will of the nation,* decrees and solemnly *proclaims that the execution of the sovereign powers* of the State of Lithuania *abolished by foreign forces in 1940, is re-established,* and henceforth Lithuania is again an independent state..." declares the Act of the Re-establishment of the State of Lithuania of 11 March 1990.

The Soviets tried to "restore constitutional order" in Latvia, Lithuania, and Estonia with the use of force. In January 1991, the Soviet military began occupying administrative buildings in Vilnius. Hundreds of thousands of people came out to protest them. Crowds surrounded military vehicles, trying to convince the soldiers not to suppress the movement for independence. The worst tragedy happened when the military tried to seize the Vilnius television tower: 14 people were shot and killed by the soldiers. Over the next few days, five more people lost their lives in Latvia. Moscow essentially retreated, not wanting to risk any more confrontations after this loss of life. The Soviet Union recognised the independence of the three republics on 9 September 1991, just a few months before its official dissolution. This step was intended to show the world that the USSR still had a modicum of control over the situation, but in reality, it represented the last agonal breaths before its final demise.

From the first moments of their renewed independence, the Baltic countries had a clear goal in mind: to return to Europe. Ultimately, this meant an uncompromising course to join the European Union and NATO. Membership in these organisations was meant to guarantee the small countries would be secure from any new aggressive actions by Russia; they never forgot how they were left to fend for themselves in 1940.

Even the one-time "fellow travellers," who came to power in the first years of re-established independence, embraced this goal. Although in Ukraine the communists and members of the Komsomol stayed in leadership positions until the mid-2000s, in the Baltic countries they hastily ceded their positions to the social-democrats, liberals, and right-centre politicians. The first president of Estonia was the writer Lennart Meri, who had lived in Europe since 1970 and held this new position from 1992 to 2001. The Baltic diaspora, quick to join the process of transformation in their homelands, came on board as consultants, members of government, and even heads of state. Latvia's President Vaira Vike-Freiberga (1999–2007) was a Canadian citizen, and both the President of Lithuania Valdas Adamkus (2004–2009) and the President of Estonia Toomas Hendrik Llves (2006–2016) were American citizens. Their backgrounds and Western values markedly sped up the reform process and the incorporation of the Baltic countries into the European Union and NATO. The question of whether people from the diaspora were "one of us" or "foreigners" never came up; not too long ago these same people were sending contraband jeans to their families.

Deregulation of the economy, lowering taxes, mass privatisation, and the break-up of outdated business affiliations at first led to hyperinflation and a sharp decline in the economy. This is the reason the first reformers are traditionally reviled. However, allowing the reforms to reach their logical conclusions permitted Latvia, Lithuania, and Estonia to witness stable economic growth at a level far exceeding that of other European countries in the 2000s and 2010s. This tendency has continued today, and has earned the countries their nickname: Baltic Tigers. In 2020, the Estonian and Latvian tax systems were awarded first and second place, respectively, in the ratings of OECD countries.

Indeed, the support of Western countries played a key role. In the 1990s, the United States and the United Kingdom put continuous pressure on Russia to pull their troops out of the Baltic countries. The Russian Federation was weakened at the time and could not retain its influence in the region. This was the ideal time for reforms and to move towards Europe.

Estonia acted boldly and took the most radical steps. The reform of its civil service deserves both respect for its decisiveness and condemnation for its "anti-democratic" methods (Europe was disturbed by those operations). In 1992, the Estonian government fired *all* of its civil servants. After reforming its government institutions, they announced a hiring of new employees. In one fell swoop they were able to fill the civil service with fresh faces, motivated to enact change. This reform ended up being the most effective instrument to fight corruption in the country, and there was no collapse of the system.

When outmoded norms are ineffective, fear of "the entire system collapsing" in their absence is not reason enough to keep them around. In 2016, Ukraine's Ministry of Health did away with Order 33, which designated typical employee rosters for medical facilities. Political and trade union cronies panicked, exclaiming, "physicians are all going to quit," "the system is going to collapse," "salaries will plummet" and so on. The catastrophe never came, hospitals did not close, and medical staff were not kicked out into the streets. What happened was the exact opposite of what had been feared: the facilities gained the ability to form their own organisational structure to best meet their needs. Deputy Minister of Health Pavlo Kovtoniuk, who served from 2016–2019, characterised the abolition of Order 33 as a step toward free-market principles for the facilities.

"As time goes by, the hospitals will get increasingly autonomous. We are giving them the instruments to optimise their work – as a way to hold on to those physicians who are best at caring for their patients."

The National Academies of Sciences of Lithuania, Latvia, and Estonia could not escape the cuts of the Baltic "scalpel." Their rigid hierarchical structure consisting of a Presidia, an exorbitant number of staff, and unnecessary real estate holdings, was irrational and in total contradiction to the spirit of the transformation underway. Many of the research staff were transferred to universities, and thousands of administrative personnel were dismissed. Unneeded real estate was sold, and the organisational structure was changed to resemble European scientific associations, with most of the funding converted to financing via grants. Scientific research gradually reoriented its focus from Russia to the West, and the number of articles published rapidly increased. The workforce at research facilities in Latvia dropped almost threefold over a two-year period – from 18,000 in 1990 to 7,000 in 1992. By 2001 there were no more than 6,000 personnel. But in the same period, the number of published articles doubled. Lithuania and Estonia went through similar transformations, and their publications increased by a factor of four.

The publications improved in quality as well as increasing in quantity. Today, articles published by Baltic researchers appear high in the rankings of most cited articles, and their impact factor increases each year. It's telling that from the late 1980s, the impact factor has had an inverse relationship with the progressive decrease in publication in Russian journals: the lower the number of articles published in Russian journals, the higher the impact factor of Baltic research papers.

In Ukraine, however, Boris Paton, head of the National Academy of Sciences for 58 years until his death at the age of 101, is praised for the fact he "saved the National Academy of Sciences of Ukraine from falling apart and being ransacked." But is it truly an achievement to save decrepit, old, needless, and redundant buildings that don't even have heat, and cannot be financially maintained? In fact, the surplus of unnecessary real estate breeds corruption. In March 2021, a doctor of technical studies and deputy director of one of the Academy's institutes, was caught taking a bribe from a private business owner. The senior employee was being paid off to (illegally) rent an unused Academy building to the businessman. The exact same story was repeated three months later at another of the Academy's institutes.

In 1991 we "declared" independence from scratch. Our historical memory of the Ukrainian National Republic was essentially destroyed, after an occupation lasting 20 years longer than that of the Baltic states, and narrowly having survived the Holodomor and Stalin's purges. In the Proclamation of Independence of Ukraine, the emphasis was on external circumstances and some abstract notion of "a thousand-year tradition of state-building."

"In view of the *mortal danger* surrounding Ukraine in connection with the state coup in the USSR on 19 August 1991;

Continuing the *thousand-year tradition of state development* in Ukraine;

Proceeding from the right of a nation to self-determination in accordance with the Charter of the United Nations and other international legal documents;

Implementing the Declaration of State Sovereignty of Ukraine, The Supreme Council (the *Verkhovna Rada*) of the Ukrainian Soviet Socialist Republic solemnly *declares* the Independence of Ukraine and the creation of an independent Ukrainian state – UKRAINE."

Were the 1990s as ideal for reforms in Ukraine as they were in the Baltic countries? It is naïve to believe they were. At the time, there was an enormous societal demand for change, and Russia was busy with countless internal issues of its own. However, we couldn't count on the same amount of support from the West, and the Ukrainian elites were more inclined to choose "stability"

In 1991 we "declared" independence from scratch. Our historical memory of the Ukrainian National Republic was essentially destroyed, after an occupation lasting 20 years longer than that of the Baltic states, and narrowly having survived the Holodomor and Stalin's purges.

over real reform. As opposed to the Baltic states, we were unable to set clearly defined goals. Legend has it that while assuming his position as Prime Minister of Ukraine in 1992, Leonid Kuchma offered the members of Parliament a proposition: "Tell me what we are building here, and I will build it for you." There was no concrete response. And so, the director of a factory built a factory.

The diaspora was never made to feel welcome in the new Ukrainian state. Many reforms were initiated, but never completed, despite the modest nature of the changes proposed. The reform of land sales and decentralisation have only just begun in the 30th year of independence, while the Baltic states completed these reforms in the first years of their renewed statehood. There is no point in comparing the progress or lack thereof made in law enforcement, the court system, and internal security. The road we have chosen to travel has proven to be longer, but in the end, it was the right one.

A massive quantity of Russian nationals flooded into the Baltic states (and into Ukraine) during Soviet times. It got so bad that in 1989 Russians in Latvia and Estonia made up a third of the population, and 10 per cent in Lithuania. Understanding Russia would manipulate the ethnic question for its own political gain, Latvia and Estonia awarded citizenship only to those who had been citizens of their countries prior to World War II, and to their progeny. They adopted the principle of ethnic rather than territorial ancestry. This principle also helped the diaspora to return swiftly and play a part in the transformation of their ancestral homeland. Russians were required to "naturalise" – that is, prove they knew the national language, history, and laws. To this day, at least a third of Russians have not taken advantage of the process and have not applied for citizenship. Meanwhile, Russia exploits this fact, declaring to the world they are being discriminated against. Unfortunately, the European Union fans the flame, complaining about "violations of human rights." Ukraine, on the other hand, adopted a "wipe the slate clean" policy and awarded Ukrainian citizenship to anyone who was living on the territory of the Ukrainian SSR, with no other requirements. The results of this policy can be seen in Ukraine's Crimean Peninsula and heard in the sound of gunfire in Eastern Ukraine today.

Swift and decisive reforms, a clear-cut path in their foreign policy, and consistent support from the West earned the Baltic states a place at the table within the European club of nations. In 2004, Latvia, Lithuania, and Estonia were granted membership to the European Union and NATO. However, it turned out their problems would not end there.

After Russia occupied a portion of Georgia in 2008 and Ukraine's Crimean Peninsula and parts of the Donbas region in 2014, and then started an ongoing Russian-Ukrainian war, the Baltic countries confronted the task of strengthening their defences. The aggression of their northern neighbour, overtly displaying its imperialistic ambitions, was a good reason to safeguard against a new annexation. The invasion could come from the west as easily as from the east since the Kaliningrad region is the most militarised area in Europe. The only physical connection between the Baltic countries and their NATO allies is a thin 104 km long sliver of land on the border of Lithuania and Poland, sandwiched between the Russian Federation and Belarus, and known as the Suwalki Gap. If the Russians capture the Gap, the defence of Latvia, Lithuania, and Estonia would become exceedingly complicated.

Even before Russia's full-scale invasion of Ukraine in February 2022, NATO had increased its deployment in the region, and the US had decided not to pull its troops out of Poland. These steps were only symbolic, but theoretically should have prevented Russia from making any ill-advised moves. Lithuania recently broadened their criteria for those who apply for government jobs to decrease the likelihood of espionage. If the applicant has family in Russia, they may very well not be hired for the position. Only time will tell if this will be enough.

Regardless of the inherent risks, the Baltic states continue to demonstrate their rejection of communist ideology to the wider world; they know all too well what it represents. In February 2021, China organised another one of its "17 + 1" summits, inviting countries from Central, Eastern, and Southern Europe. The meeting was designed to lobby the economic, political, and cultural interests of China on the European continent, including advancing the New Silk Road initiative. Poland's President personally attended the summit, while Estonia and Latvia only sent their Ministers of Foreign Affairs. The most notable slap in the face in Beijing came from Lithuania, however, who sent their Minister of Transportation to the summit and have since left the "17 + 1" group. In July 2021, the Lithuanian government gave the go-ahead for Taiwan to open a representative office in Vilnius. Lithuania and China have already withdrawn their respective ambassadors since communist China unconditionally regards Taiwan as part of their territory.

Ukraine has not yet adopted such a principled stand. The proposed but unrealized sale of the aircraft turbine manufacturing company Motor Sich to the Chinese in 2017–2018 created a political scandal. The first president of Ukraine, Leonid Kravchuk, had remained a communist in theory and in practice; since 2006 he had served as Honorary President of the "Ukraine-China" Society founded by the oligarch Hryhoriy Surkis. In this role, Kravchuk travelled to China at the invitation of the Central Committee of the Communist Party of China in October 2017. A year later he "highly praised" the strategy of the Nineteenth National Congress of the Chinese Communist Party. Davyd Arakhamia, the leader of the Servant of the People faction in the Ukrainian Parliament, was so taken with the wisdom of Xi Jinping, he personally assisted in the translation into Ukrainian and publication of the Chinese leader's book on governance. One of the chapters of the book is titled "Carry on the Enduring Spirit of Mao Zedong Thought." The Cultural Revolution, just one expression of Mao's *enduring spirit*, cost the Chinese people 20 million lives alone.

To better understand how China regards Ukraine, you only need look at the official

website of the Chinese Embassy in Ukraine, where no Ukrainian language version of the site exists. There are a few news items written in Ukrainian, but the rest of the site is in Chinese and Russian. However, this has not stopped Sergey Shefir, one of Ukrainian President Volodymyr Zelensky's top aides, from selling the rights to broadcast a cartoon series "Gulliver's Return," produced by Zelensky's comedy studio Kvartal 95, on Chinese television. The official signing ceremony in September 2021 was attended by the Chinese Ambassador to Ukraine Fan Xianrong. It's hard to imagine something similar happening in Lithuania, Ukraine's fellow victim of communist occupation.

A clear position on controversial issues is a trait of a mature society. Ukraine has not held such a stance for centuries, let alone for the last 30 years. We certainly lacked the fortitude to make complex and unpopular decisions, and these weaknesses were adroitly manipulated by Russia, though not as successfully as they would have hoped. In the end, the Orange Revolution and the Revolution of Dignity triumphed in Ukraine. The more time goes by, the more the following idiom is solidified: when you strike out at one Ukrainian, five more will greet the aggressor. Today this new cultural phenomenon is our collective response that puts to rest the mythical slogan: "I live on the outskirts of town, and I don't want to get involved." And this is a dramatic change to the concept inherited from the 1990s. In this we have become more like our Baltic friends. We are moving forward, albeit with obstacles in our path, but at least we are moving in the right direction.

The full-scale invasion of Russia into Ukraine beginning on 24 February 2022 did not surprise a lot of people. But none of the "experts" believed a mass resistance

against the world's second largest army would arise, led by a mailman from the Ukrainian Postal Service, an ex-bartender, and even an old lady armed with only a jar of pickles. The strength demonstrated by Ukrainians in Kharkiv, Sumy, Chernihiv, Mykolayiv, Berdyansk, Melitopol, Mariupol, and many other cities, small towns, and residential areas, has already nullified the false narrative about "two Ukraines" created by Russian political consultants. There is no East or West Ukraine. There are no cities that have "Russian" or "Halytsky" culture. There is only one Ukraine. The one with its own place on the map. The one with the chance to end the struggle against the *russkiy mir* (Russian World) that has been slithering its way into Ukraine for centuries. The one Ukraine fighting a real war for independence right now, incinerating the Russians like nobody has ever been able to do until now, with righteous fire.

"History is written by the victors" is a quote attributed to Napoleon. And it is fair. Ukrainian history textbooks were composed in Moscow for a very long time. Regardless of what they fabricated there, the nation's collective memory is more powerful. It is what drives our actions in the war today. On 8 March 2022, Ukrainian poet Serhiy Zhadan, who has never abandoned his beloved hometown of Kharkiv, wrote on Twitter: "History is not only being rewritten today – it is being rewritten in the Ukrainian language," by the Victorious.

Liberty Avenue (or Laisves Aleya) in Kaunas has not changed much with the passage of time. Although its facades are now well-groomed and freshly painted, the same two- or three-story cosy buildings that student Romas Kalanta would have passed by remain. Today, dozens of cafes and restaurants serving local and international cuisine have replaced the Konditerija. The aroma of coffee, pizza, and perfume are now mixed in with the smell of baking bread. The exhaust fumes from Zhyhuli have disappeared.

An eyewitness to Kalanta's death, Romualdas Balchis, in an interview with the Lithuanian media *15 Min*, could not confirm Romas yelled out "Glory to Lithuania!" right before he lit himself on fire. Whether it is fact or a historical myth, the 19-year-old student continues to symbolise the fight of

the Baltic states for the re-establishment of their independence. It was not mere coincidence he chose the location of his act of protest as an avenue not far from the Musical Theatre, where in 1940 the "People's Council" was forced to vote, under the barrel of a gun, to approve the incorporation of Lithuania into the USSR.

Romas Kalanta's self-immolation on 14 May 1972 has been commemorated in Lithuania as a national holiday since 2002. That was the year a memorial, the "Field of Victims," created by sculptors Robertas Antinis and Saulus Juskis, was dedicated on the site of Kalanta's act of protest. The cast iron sheets embedded in the ground represent the pages of history damaged by the flames. They are accompanied by 19 stones commemorating every year of Kalanta's life. Today, on this date each year, schoolchildren in the once-again independent Lithuania place flowers at the memorial. They pay tribute to their fellow student with a moment of silence, and sing songs by the Beatles, Led Zeppelin, Bob Dylan, and Jimi Hendrix, among others.

"There must be some kind of way outta here..." are the first words of Bob Dylan's song "All Along the Watchtower" (1967), released five years before Romas Kalanta's protest. It is highly likely Romas heard that song, and wrestled with the same question. Ukrainians, it seems, have discovered the answer.

w

The Spectre of Smuta
The Entertainment Industry of Russian Irredentism
A Working Woman's Story
The Adventures of Russian Propagandists
Deus ex Ucraina: The Lost Ones
Hammer + Sickle = Death + Famine
Mature Ukraine

The Black Sea WHALE

A Beacon in the Sea of Troubles

Mapping Russia's Devolution

Story by Janusz Bugajski
Illustrated by Olenka Zahorodnyk

THE RUPTURE OF THE RUSSIAN Federation will be the third phase of imperial collapse, following the unravelling of the Soviet bloc, and the disintegration of the Soviet Union in the early 1990s. It will also herald another "time of troubles" *(smutnoie vremya):* a period of political crisis and chaos Muscovite Russia experienced in the late 16th and early 17th centuries and was replicated during the disintegration of Tsarist Russia in World War I. However, unlike in the 17th and 20th centuries, modern-day Moscow lacks the capacity and geopolitical opportunity to reconstitute Russia as a continental empire.

The Russian Federation, the inheritor of Moscow's remaining dominions, is a failed state with an incomplete national identity. It has proved unable to transform itself into a nation-state, a civic state, or even an effective imperial state. Russia's numerous weaknesses are exacerbated by a convergence of factors, including dependence on export revenues based predominantly on fossil fuels, a contracting economy with little prospect of growth or global competitiveness, and intensifying regional and ethnic disquiet. Russia's full-scale invasion of Ukraine in February 2022 accelerated the process of state rupture by failing to achieve the Kremlin's stated goals, resulting in substantial military casualties, and damaging international economic sanctions.

Although Russia's 1993 Constitution defines the country as a federation, it is, in reality, a centralised neo-imperial construct, integrated on the basis of administrative proclamation, and not voluntary agreement. The artificial state is approaching the end of a regime cycle in which the political status quo is becoming increasingly precarious. Not since the fracturing of the Soviet Union have several simultaneous crises become so stark, from the government's inability to ensure sustained economic development to widening disparities between Moscow and the federal regions. Add to that the deepening distrust of Moscow's governance, the limited efficacy of mass repression, and a looming military defeat or indefinite quagmire in Ukraine, and the situation looks even more unstable.

Intensifying Pressures

To prolong its survival, Russia needs to develop into a genuine federation. Yet instead of pursuing decentralisation to accommodate the aspirations of distinct ethnic and regional interests, the Russian government is engaged in wholesale restrictions. Resentments have mounted over Moscow's unilateral appointment of regional governors and its appropriation of local resources. Its inadequate response to the COVID-19 pandemic and other national emergencies, as well as mounting casualties in the war against Ukraine, particularly among non-Russian populations, have added to the feelings of discontent. Although the regime is obsessed with preventing or quelling protests, simultaneous crises in several far-flung regions can overwhelm Moscow's repressive apparatus, or its ability to provide economic relief to control unrest.

The Kremlin fears any repetition of the "colour revolutions" which shook Ukraine and Georgia, where corrupt authoritarian governments were toppled because they could no longer prevent public protests against election fraud. Mass demonstrations in Belarus in the summer of 2020, over blatant vote rigging, disproved the conventional wisdom about a passive Belarusian public – a theory mirrored by the widely held image of Russian citizens. Although protests in Belarus were eventually extinguished, the root causes of public unrest were not addressed. Demonstrations and attacks on government buildings in Kazakhstan in January 2022 served as another warning to Moscow that simmering public anger can explode suddenly and spread rapidly. The appearance of stability cannot be taken for granted, and a triggering event such as price increases or forged elections can ignite public demands for broader political change.

The Russian Federation confronts an urgent existential paradox. This will become starker as the closure of Vladimir Putin's presidential term approaches, regardless of whether it is constitutionally extended through rigged elections. Centralisation and repression without sustained economic growth will increase public opposition and generate turmoil, while liberalisation and decentralisation would also result in the unravelling of the state. Without political pluralism, economic reform, and regional autonomy, the federal structure will become increasingly unmanageable. However, even if democratic reforms were undertaken, several regions could use the opportunity to secede. The chances for violent conflicts may diminish in the event of systemic reform, while the potential for violent conflict substantially increases if reforms are indefinitely blocked.

As the country slides toward domestic turmoil, the existing federal system will be viewed as illegitimate by expanding sectors of the population. A spectrum of domestic scenarios can then materialise to thrust the country toward fragmentation. Intensifying intra-elite power struggles, escalating conflicts between the Kremlin and regional governments, factional strife in the state security and military *(siloviki)* institutions, and a breakdown of central controls in several parts of the country all have the potential to drive this shift.

The power structure in the multi-national federation is more fragile than that of the Soviet Union, due to an over-reliance on the persona of an individual leader, and no predictable and legitimate method of succession. Additionally, Russia no longer possesses an all-encompassing Communist Party apparatus that can ensure a relatively seamless change of leadership. A democratic transition through competitive elections is anathema to the ruling clique, as it would stimulate even more uncertainty over Russia's future. In fact, the emergence of a democratic system after Putin's demise may be less feasible now than it was in the 1990s. Expectations for genuine state-wide democracy are low, institutions are hollow, alternative political parties are weak, and civil society is repressed. It would take time

RUSSKAYA
Русская
История
RUSSIAN HISTO

for a coherent political elite to emerge at an all-state level, and such a process can be challenged and derailed by autocratic, nationalist, and populist forces.

A much more likely prospect is a move to deepen fissures, grow challenges to the hierarchy of power, weaken central controls, and widen political divisions. National identities and ethnic divisions can fuel separatism, but secessionist sentiments can also develop within the same ethnos, where distinct regions harbour an assortment of grievances against the central government or calculate that separation would be economically beneficial. Initial challenges to state integrity can be gradual and non-violent, although violent scenarios cannot be discounted. It can result in the full separation of some federal units and the amalgamation of others into new federal or confederal structures.

Moves toward separation by any of the 21 ethnic republics are likely to provoke demands for self-determination among several regions with ethnic Russian majorities. This would significantly weaken the centre and lessen the likelihood of maintaining an autocratic state. Instructively, in the early 1990s when the Soviet Union began to unravel, 40 per cent of the predominantly ethnic Russian regions pressed for greater autonomy, and some veered toward sovereignty similar to the ethnic republics. Enhanced regional activism can be a bargaining tactic for extracting finances or other resources from the Centre. However, separatist movements often start with demands for economic decentralisation and then escalate in response to central government actions as well as soaring elite and public aspirations.

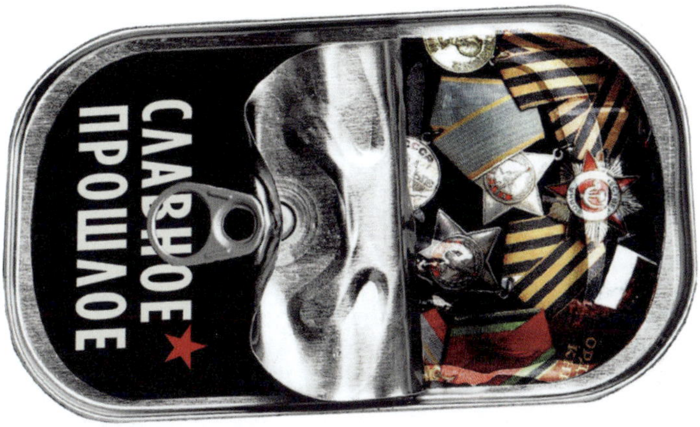

Triggers for Turmoil

A key driver of state disintegration would be a military defeat or a prolonged military stalemate for which the Kremlin is widely blamed domestically. Increasingly, public acquiescence and regime survival under Putin's rule has been based on an aggressive foreign policy, territorial revisionism, patriotic militarism, and anti-Western propaganda. A major setback or stalemate in Ukraine involving significant casualties will invoke opposition to Putin's policies, propel power struggles to replace him, stimulate popular revolts against a discredited leadership, and highlight the accumulated failures of the state. The Tsarist empire collapsed during a war with imperial Germany in World War I, and the Soviet empire disintegrated in the wake of a failed war in Afghanistan. Vladislav Surkov, the Kremlin's former chief ideologist, may have been correct when he claimed, in an article published in November 2021, that if Russia does not engage in successful imperial expansion, then it will expire as a state.

Russia's leaders are also fearful of spontaneous public unrest, as witnessed in their overreactions to peaceful street protests, and constant attempts to eliminate all forms of organised opposition. Officials are aware public opinion polls are not a failsafe barometer of the public mood. They tend to be sparse in many regions of the country, and often reflect an unwillingness to reveal genuine sentiments. The results of these polls can also swing in unpredictable directions during times of escalating crisis and perceived regime fragility. Additionally, as elections results are falsified by state actors, the public's political preferences cannot be accurately gauged by state officials – thus contributing to anxieties within the "power vertical" over the longevity of the

current system. What appears to be apathy, avoidance, and even feelings of hopelessness among the majority can rapidly spiral into hatred and aggression toward the authorities.

There are many factors with the ability to spread and fuel disruption, and unrest can be triggered by either a major event or a series of rolling crises. Such catalysts can have strong economic dimensions with a wide array of public grievances, such as a deepening depression, rampant inflation, wage arrears, inadequate housing, environmental destruction, collapsing infrastructures, declining social services, and swift spikes in unemployment. Kremlin assurances that economic downturns are merely temporary phenomena will ring increasingly hollow if they are prolonged and felt deeply. Even the traditionally pro-government elderly population and residents of small cities, towns, and rural areas will feel increasingly abandoned and cheated by Moscow. Local political actors will accuse the federal government of economic exploitation and highlight the parasitism and arbitrariness of state bureaucrats' existence at the expense of public well-being. Although protests could be spontaneous and initially small-scale, they can also snowball and combine numerous single-issue campaigns.

The Putin regime has spent the last two decades convincing citizens there is no viable alternative to the prevailing system. Nonetheless, the relationship between protests and economic conditions can become combustible when society experiences constant decline and not simply "stagnation;" when inequalities between rich and poor become increasingly conspicuous; and where official mismanagement and corruption are rampant. To avert a revolutionary scenario, the administration may impose a variety of measures, including the provision of urgent economic benefits for key sectors of the population or a mass crackdown in one or more regions. A programme of limited decentralisation may also be attempted to pacify public unrest. The limits of republican and regional sovereignty would be tested in trying to forge a workable federation, and several regions will see an opportunity for pursuing maximalist options during a period of confusion at the central level.

Attempts to pacify the most volatile areas of the country through economic incentives could boomerang. Selective economic benefits can provoke resentment in other regions and convince people that mass opposition to Kremlin policy can be lucrative in increasing state funding. Political concessions to local leaders and administrative devolution will encourage governors to act more independently and push for more extensive autonomy. Increased resources and authority for ethnic republics could also inflame Russian ethnic nationalism, driven by animosity against national republics such as those in the North Caucasus perceived to be favoured by Moscow. This can either increase calls for greater centralisation and the elimination of ethnic republics, or provoke demands for the creation of a distinct Russian ethno-national republic.

The regime's ability to impose mass repression across the country, or even in several restless regions simultaneously, will prove inadequate. Strikes and other forms of industrial labour action can break out across several regions with employees protesting low or unpaid wages, poor working conditions, rising prices, and falling living standards. Spiralling chaos will witness ebbs and flows of mass protests and police repression. Police attacks on peaceful manifestations can engender radicalisation and more violent responses. Protests will also provide opportunities for coordination between different movements, causes, and locations. A revolutionary situation will develop when the state is incapable of maintaining the repression necessary to subdue all public unrest, while a growing number of people are unwilling to live under a failed dictatorial regime amidst deepening poverty.

The Kremlin will also attempt to steer the population toward ethnic scapegoating by depicting a potentially separatist republic as an existential threat to Russia and its citizens. This would replicate how Chechnya was demonised by officials when Prime Minister Putin launched the second war of reconquest in August 1999. However, the promotion of ethnic and religious hatreds would further break down national and social cohesion and convince sizeable segments of the Muslim populations Russia had become their existential threat. Moscow will not be able to sustain state survival if it scapegoats specific nations and alienates ethnic groups. Such a policy may also prove politically counter-productive by convincing the majority of Russia's citizens that separatist entities should be allowed to secede to avoid bloodshed. The classic "divide and rule" strategy can thereby result in more division and less rule.

Looming Power Struggles

Before the federal structure begins to rupture, Russia will face a prolonged spiral of chaos and ungovernability, and accelerating elite power struggles in which state institutions witness a breakdown in the chain of command, as was evident in the final months of the Soviet Union. Some institutions may cease to function altogether, while regional and central elites compete more vigorously over shrinking financial resources. Kremlin fears come to fruition regarding the enduring loyalty of elites who have benefited from presidential control over state assets. Their adherence will dissipate alongside their shrinking economic benefits, and this could herald a series of turf battles, kidnappings, assassinations, and attempts to use the security forces against political and business rivals.

Russia's political stability revolves around an elite consensus in supporting Putin together with sufficient public acquiescence. It is not dependent on popular legitimacy or enduring institutions. Putin has managed to balance competing political, economic, and security factions, while relying on his security service connections and the allegiance of his original Leningrad inner circle. Internal power struggles are unlikely to produce a clear winner, whether a reformer or another centralising autocrat. They are more likely to be prolonged, violent, and inconclusive. Putin's ouster will not necessarily end the struggle for power or pacify public protests. On the contrary, it will intensify political battles and popular revolts, because there is little trust among top officials and minimal public confidence in the ruling elite.

Power struggles can erupt between rival political "clans" or networks. The strongest of these "clans" include state security officials and military personnel *(siloviki)*, heads of state corporations, major oligarchs (tycoons), leaders of loyal political parties, industrial lobbies, and regional heads. These conflicts can burst into the open once the consensus around Putin begins to unravel or if the country faces protracted economic decline and growing competition for scarcer resources. Contests between political rivals to replace Putin will undermine the "power vertical" and solidify factions within the internal security forces. Police officers in some regions are likely to remain neutral or even join public protests once demonstrations expand. Paradoxically, substantial sectors of the population who supported Putin, because he ensured order and predictability, will abandon the regime when it appears to be increasingly weak and yielding. When uncertainty and chaos spread in the country and no credible successor emerges in Moscow, sectors of society will look toward local and regional leaders to restore some semblance of order in their cities and regions.

Elite loyalty toward the Kremlin is not based on shared ideology but on raw economic and political advantages. Elements of the elite will lose confidence in the regime if resources for corruption become depleted, international isolation curtails revenues, and social unrest spreads. With a shrinking national economic "pie," the pyramid of state paternalism favouring specific interest groups will become increasingly unstable. A conflict within the elite can materialise over diminishing resources, with some individuals seeking to steer social unrest against their rivals. The ruling United Russia political party can splinter, as many regional members of the party did not enlist because of ideological affiliation or political loyalty, but for opportunistic reasons, and are likely to abandon it when power struggles weaken the central government. The systemic opposition parties, including the Communists and Liberal Democrats, can adopt a more independent posture in criticising the Kremlin if their benefits dwindle. Regional branches of party organisations have also proven to be less compliant than national bodies and could break away or challenge Moscow loyalists. This can lead to factionalism, purges, and outright conflicts within the ruling strata.

In the midst of an unsuccessful war and with a shrinking economy, a coalition of high officials and security chiefs may stage a "palace coup" and blame the incumbent regime for Russia's problems. Nevertheless, such a rotation of the "power vertical" will do little for economic development and can increase social turmoil and even trigger civil conflicts and insurrections. Political factions in Moscow may seek allies among regional elites, as was the case during the Soviet breakdown in the early 1990s. Both Gorbachev and Yeltsin encouraged regional sovereignty to weaken their rival's position and enhance their support base. Renewed attempts to manipulate republican and regional leaders will become another precursor for the dissolution of the state.

As power struggles intensify, Russia's military commanders will become increasingly alienated from the Kremlin. This would become especially evident if the armed forces were mobilised to pacify public unrest. During state collapse, the military can also experience a breakdown in the chain of command, fractures along ethnic and religious lines, clashes between different ethnicities, and the evacuation of non-Russians from service outside their federal regions. Military casualties in the war against Ukraine demonstrate that non-Russians are significantly overrepresented, largely because the military offers poorer populations career prospects. Moscow has also sought to deflect blame for war crimes on national minorities in the Russian military in the pursuit of a "divide and conquer" approach to absolve ethnic Russians of genocide. Nonetheless, the deployment of other nations as cannon fodder in a foreign war will intensify anger against Moscow, and military defeats in Ukraine will make Russian armed forces more prone to conflicts and mutinies. As the federal crisis deepens and the military fractures, various weapons will be acquired by militias, insurgents, and emerging proto-states.

Regional Revivals

As turmoil spreads, a regional resurgence will be evident across the country. Russia's "federal vertical" is fragile, as it remains dependent on co-opting the loyalty of power elites in a limited number of key regions – either those with sizeable populations or with key industries and resources, particularly in the energy field. The stability of the federal structure will come under increasing pressure, especially when central control weakens because of elite conflicts and budgetary contractions that severely undercut subsidies to the federal subjects. Governors can seek popular legitimacy in their home territories by opting for regional sovereignty. Some governors will also conclude that Moscow's campaign against titular languages in the republics and plans for regional amalgamation will further reduce their authority, and even lead to disbanding republican institutions, as well as subjecting them more directly to Moscow. Such developments will raise support among governors and local legislatures for sovereignty and self-determination.

Demands in the ethnic republics and Russian-majority regions will be driven by an accumulation of grievances, including sharp rises in poverty levels, declines in federal financial subsidies, deteriorating local infrastructure, and costly and inadequate transportation connections between cities. Contested land use between federal and regional authorities, an absence of environmental protection, deteriorating health care services, and the neglect of significant historical sites add to the list, alongside harmful social policies, police brutality, rampant official corruption, and overall public alienation from central decision-making. Simultaneously, expectations of material benefits, rising ethno-national status, and international recognition could provide positive energisation if Moscow's overlordship is eliminated.

Disparities in regional self-assertion are likely, with leaders in ethnically homogenous republics and resource rich regions, or entities more geographically distant from the capital, escalating their demands and fortifying links with nearby foreign states. Regional activists will mount challenges to

the legal basis of the federal state and the position of its subjects. Some could seek the full application of federalism or propose new structural arrangements to loosen ties with Moscow, including a confederation or commonwealth. The wealthier regions with greater economic potential and a sizeable export portfolio will demand a radical reduction of the money transferred to the central government or may withhold payments. This can be the case with oil-producing regions in Western Siberia or the mineral-rich republic of Sakha.

Power will devolve to the regions when the Moscow-centred vertical begins to splinter. In the event of major public unrest, regional governors will find themselves in an untenable position. The Kremlin will demand they suppress local protests, while citizens will press them to fulfil their regional responsibilities. Attempts by regional authorities to use local protests as bargaining chips to gain resources from Moscow may no longer bear fruit if the Centre cannot afford to comply, and protests escape the control of local officials. Governors can either avoid a crackdown or blame Moscow for a harsh repressive response. Either way, they will fortify local public opinion against the Centre. The process will expose the deep-rooted regional resentments against Russia's capital, which is widely viewed as a colonial exploiter with an irredeemably corrupt bureaucracy. People will become more inclined to identify themselves as residents of a particular region rather than as citizens of an integral Russian state.

Some republican and regional leaders will claim discrimination in the federal structure and push for genuine autonomy. In a similar manner to that of federal Yugoslavia on the eve of its disintegration in the early 1990s, several richer regions will voice their resentment at subsidising the poorer ones, while claiming they would be better managed and more prosperous if either they separated from the federation or the poorer republics such as the North Caucasus seceded. Separatist movements that contributed to the crumbling of the Soviet communist empire in the 1990s were partly or

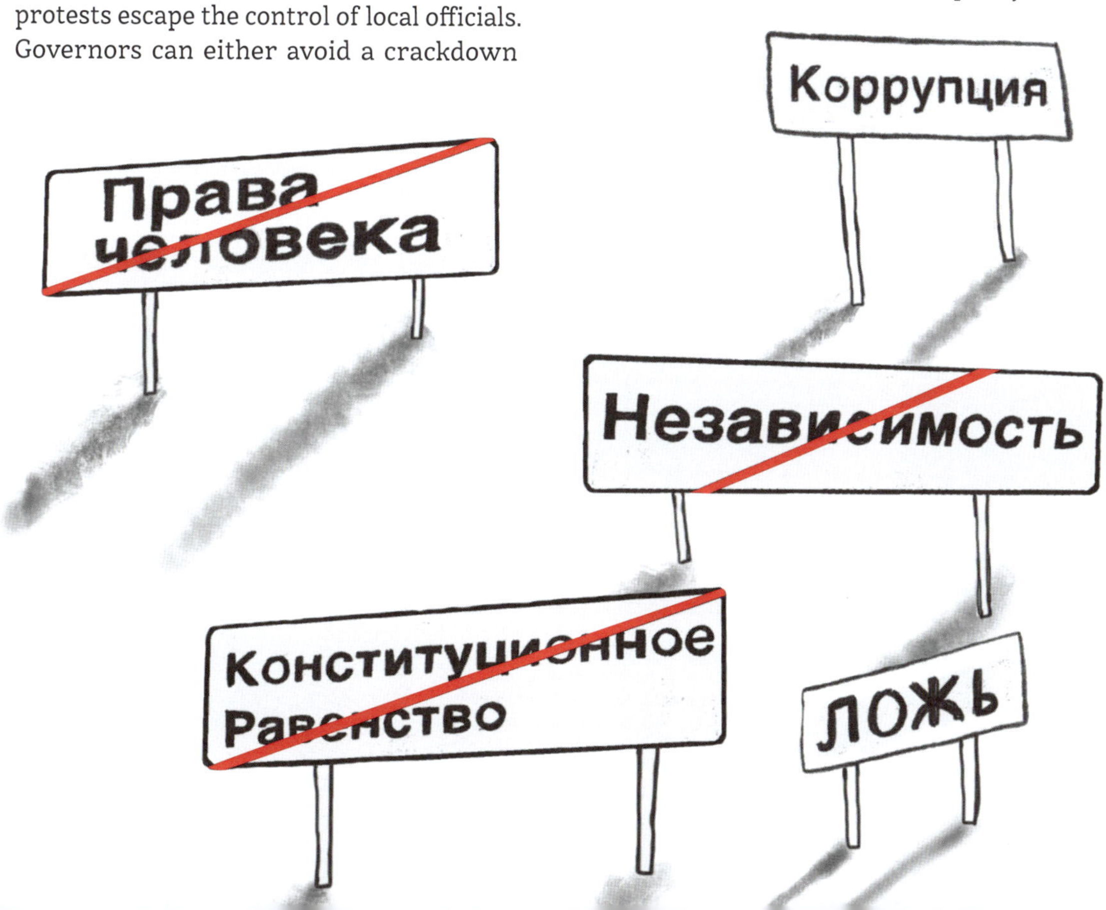

initially elite projects designed to keep more resources in the hands of Union Republics. Many leaders of republican pro-independence movements emerged from the Soviet establishment.

Regional elites will conclude the costs of maintaining loyalty to Moscow outweigh the benefits and will opt for greater regional sovereignty. When local elites no longer trust the Kremlin to ensure their political legitimacy and provide necessary resources, they will promote their own power base as authentic republican or regional leaders. Public movements and local authorities in different republics, *krais,* and *oblasts* can synchronise their demands toward Moscow once the hierarchy of power splinters, and they may form cross-regional linkages for mutual support. A knock-on effect would be visible, whereby the success of some federal subjects in gaining greater sovereignty without central government intervention encourages other republic and regions to push for fuller autonomy. Moscow's traditionally divisive policies to provoke conflicts between ethnic groups and disorient the opposition will prove less successful where ethnic republican leaders seek coalitions with representatives of different national groups and assist other entities in pushing for sovereignty.

Republican leaders will also demand control over natural resources and economic assets on their territories, insisting that they have been unfairly exploited by Moscow. Even some ethnic districts, such as the Khanty-Mansi Autonomous *Okrug* – Yugra in the Tyumen *Oblast*, can claim sole ownership over natural resources in regions supplying a substantial proportion of Russia's oil and natural gas revenues. As the federation loosens, regional governments will stake claims to a variety of economic benefits, including export privileges, tax reductions, and special quotas for local products, as well as direct access to pipelines exporting oil and gas currently controlled at the federal level.

Russia will undergo a revival of many of the pro-independence movements which

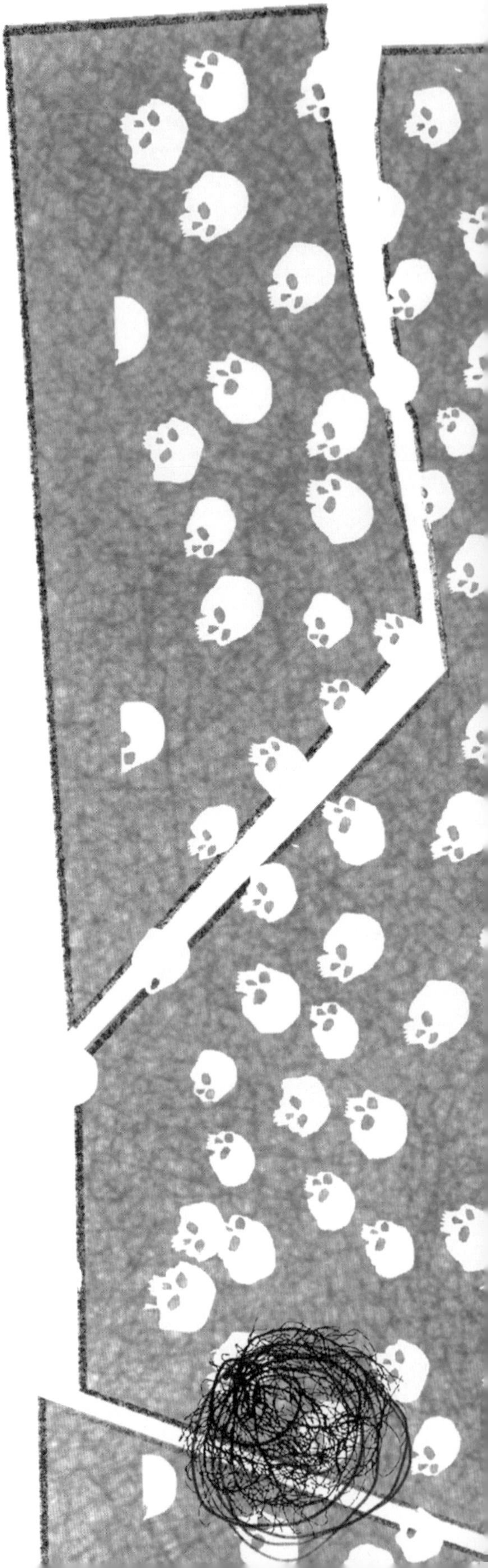

ГОЙДА!
ЕДИНАЯ РОССИЯ

emerged during the collapse of the Soviet Union. In several cases, members of titular ethnic groups will claim the right to play a more dominant role in their republics. Numerous ethnicities can assert indigenous status and residential longevity in their home territories, distinct from recent ethnic Russian or other settlers. Ethnic activists will also challenge the dominant Muscovite narrative that all republics voluntary entered the Tsarist Empire, the Soviet Union, or the Russian Federation. Ethnic elites will seek public support by asserting for the smaller nations the republics are their only homeland, whereas Russians possess a much larger territory outside these republics. Such pronouncements could lead to pressures on members of non-titular groups – particularly ethnic Russians – to leave the republics.

Inter-ethnic frictions, inter-religious disputes, and even violent clashes can be expected in some parts of the country. During a period of economic decline and political uncertainty, an assortment of ethnonationalist movements will emerge, with some seeking scapegoats to mobilise the public. Members of several non-titular ethnic groups will raise complaints that republican elites have promoted their own nations at the cost of other ethnicities and engaged in minority assimilation. Such allegations could be most evident in the overlapping historical, territorial, and resource claims in the North Caucasus and these belief systems can strengthen aspirations toward both the separation and fracturing of some republics.

The Kremlin is mindful of promoting Russian ethno-nationalism domestically to dampen discontent over the deteriorating economy, as this would contribute to tearing the country apart. Fanning xenophobia, racism, Islamophobia, and anti-immigrant sentiments could light a fuse Moscow will be unable to extinguish. Surveys have consistently indicated ethnocentric and xenophobic sentiments are widespread in the country and have been bolstered by anti-immigrant attitudes against workers from Central Asia and the North Caucasus. However, the exploitation of such sentiments by state actors and a growth in Russian ethnonationalism will provoke anti-Russian sentiments among other nationalities.

According to the 2010 census, Russia's population stood at 142.9 million. About one fifth (nearly 30 million people) belong to non-Russian nationalities, and the proportion has been steadily rising. The demographic decline of ethnic Russians poses challenges for the country's social, political, and territorial cohesion and will encourage movements for autonomy, secession, and independence. According to census figures between 1989 and 2010, in 14 of the 21 republics (excluding the occupied Ukrainian Crimean Peninsula) the ethnic-Russian population has consistently decreased proportionally to the titular nationality. In 13 republics, ethnic Russians form less than half of the total population. In nine republics, ethnic Russians form less than a third of the total population. In 11 republics, the ethnic-Russian population is smaller than that of the titular nationality. Additionally, regional identities in Siberia, the Urals, the Pacific region, and elsewhere, have also been consolidated and will motivate calls for statehood regardless of common origin and language, as witnessed in the former British colonies.

Rupture Scenarios

An initial rupture of the state could involve a limited fracture. Amid economic distress and political chaos, the separation of one or more federal entities can occur where there is little prospect of reconciliation with Moscow. In this scenario, the Kremlin accepts such an outcome to avoid mass violence which could spread to other republics and regions. Chechnya is a primary candidate for such a fracture because the foundations of a separate state already exist, and independence was initially achieved during the 1990s. Other republics may declare their sovereignty without moving toward outright secession or they may seek to emulate Chechnya's example, especially in the North Caucasus or the Middle Volga. This could resemble the situation in 1990 when all autonomous republics in the RSFSR proclaimed their sovereignty, although stopping short of secession.

Some regions with a predominantly ethnic Russian population may also demand the status of autonomous republics. This would include *krais* and *oblasts* objecting to an asymmetrical federation amidst growing calls for self-administration and sovereignty in parts of Siberia and the Pacific region. A more widespread fragmentation would occur once the regime itself begins to unravel at the centre through intense power battles. This could be sparked by Putin's incapacitation, assassination, side-lining, or sudden natural death. In the less violent scenario, a reformist or quasi-democratic leadership takes over the presidency and even includes some members of the political opposition to placate a frustrated public. However, a rival coup attempt may also be staged by hard-liners seeking to preserve the political structure and either maintain Putin at the helm or replace him with a similar authoritarian figure. Such a scenario would be reminiscent of the failed seizure of power by Soviet hard-liners in August 1991 that triggered the collapse of the Soviet Union. A coup by Russian statist-imperialists would be resisted in several ethno-national republics, as well as in Moscow and Saint Petersburg, although some regional authorities may decide to wait until there is a clearer outcome.

The federal structure will be a casualty of Russia's intra-elite battles. However, administrative ruptures may not affect the entire country uniformly. Some federal units can push for secession and others for extensive autonomy and confederation. At some critical point, the Kremlin could decide on violent centralisation and mass repression to keep the country intact, and this itself would trigger violent responses in several parts of the federation. If passive resistance fails to dislodge the regime, then one viable option will be armed resistance – whether through urban warfare or armed partisan movements in the more disaffected regions. In driving the opposition underground, the regime will radicalise several groups who may turn to sabotage, bombings, and assassinations to further disrupt state authority. The Kremlin may endeavour to mobilise the public through a major military intervention in a rebel republic, claiming it had embarked on "anti-Russian separatism" and endangered the country's territorial integrity. However, public opinion could prove lukewarm to another military confrontation, and citizens will prefer several republics secede to avoid a prolonged domestic war in the wake of the massive military losses in Ukraine.

In some parts of the country, the collapse of central power and a vacuum in regional authority could lead to local security personnel, armed militias, or crime groups seizing control over regional governments and local economies. Alternatively, regional authorities can demand the withdrawal of Russian troops, and in some republics and regions local governors will establish their own military and security units to defend the fledgling states – following a similar model to the creation of armed forces in the early 1990s in the former Union Republics and in the separatist enclaves within Moldova, Georgia, and Azerbaijan.

During prolonged turmoil, both Russian ethno-nationalism and statist-imperialism will witness a resurgence and mobilise supporters, just as ethnic and regional separatism mushrooms throughout the country. Russian nationalists and imperialists could challenge the central government as well as several regional administrations. Some nationalist leaders may marshal pro-regime groups to prevent state fracture, or they may seek to replace the government with a more explicitly imperialist or ethno-nationalist regime which can salvage state integrity and eliminate opponents. Nationalists can establish militia groups on the pretext of defending Russian ethnics in various republics, resisting regional independence movements, and preventing a meltdown of the state. The conflict will be intensified by religious differences between Muslim and Orthodox populations exploited by militants on both sides.

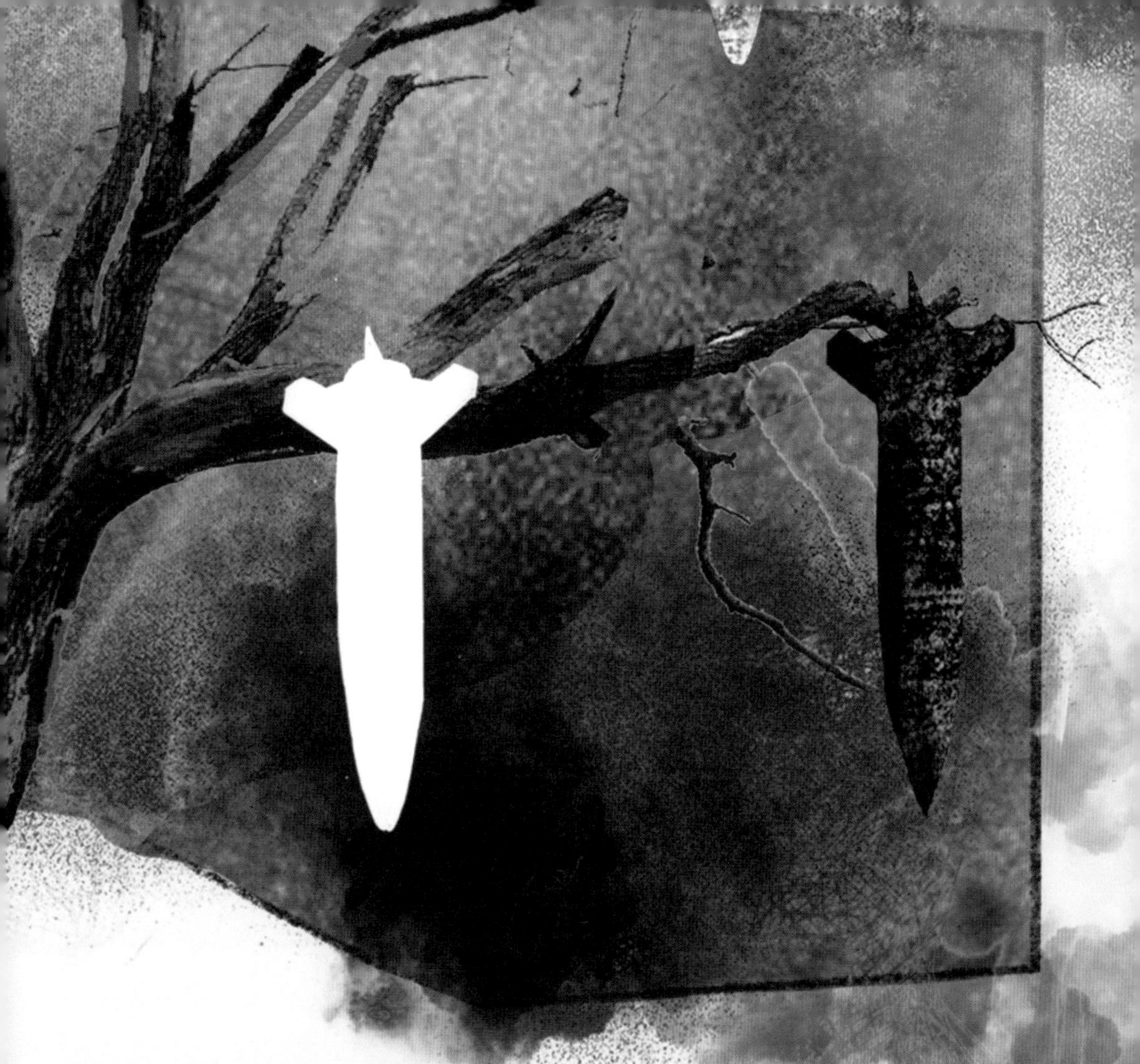

Emerging National States

In a scenario of escalating state disintegration, Moscow's attempts to subdue revolt sparks broader resistance across Russia between protestors and security forces, resulting in conflicts spreading to numerous regional capitals. Security and military units will become thinly stretched and unable to contain a multiplicity of political revolts. The 1990s demonstrated when Russia's central government weakens and power struggles intensify, numerous republics and regions reach for sovereignty and even independence to provide a measure of stability. Political paralysis at the federal centre will encourage several republics and regions to issue declarations of independence and organise public referendums. Movements toward self-determination in richer and more economically developed republics such as Tatarstan and Bashkortostan will encourage similar initiatives in neighbouring republics. They can voice a spectrum of demands for their future status, including sovereignty, confederation, or outright independence. Such assertions will have a domino effect throughout the country and stimulate other republics and regions to emulate their success.

Several nations will assert historical precedents for statehood by highlighting periods of independence before Russia's imperial conquest. These include Tatars, Bashkorts, Karelians, Udmurts, Moksha, Erzya, Mari, Circassians, Balkars, Chechens, Ingush, Kalmyks, Khakass, Altais, Buryats, Tuvans, and Sakha. Activists in multiple other nations in the High North, Siberia, and the Pacific region can demand their own autonomous regions with greater control over territories and resources, including oil, natural gas, gold, uranium, and other minerals. A number of indigenous peoples can claim the right to self-determination under the United Nations Charter and the 2017 UN Declaration on the Rights of Indigenous Peoples. They will affirm legal rights to their traditional territories and resources and to administrative self-determination. They could proceed further by asserting statehood, according to the UN General Assembly 1960 Declaration on the Granting of Independence to Colonial Countries and Peoples. Even nations in Russian-majority *krais* and *oblasts* can claim indigenous status prior to the Russian conquest and colonisation as grounds for self-determination and independence.

The Federation can unravel along regional lines as well as ethno-republican boundaries.

Russian ethno-nationalists will claim Russians have been discriminated against in the USSR and the Russian Federation and need their own single national republic or a federation of Russian republics. Residents of resource-rich regions or with strong local identities could push for independence based on inclusive multi-ethnic principles. Some predominantly ethnic Russian regions have previously created the rudiments of statehood and such initiatives can be revived. The most notable case was the short-lived Urals Republic in 1993, consisting of six *oblasts:* Sverdlovsk, Perm, Chalyabinsk, Tyumen, Kurgan, and Orenburg. Other Russian majority regions can emerge by default as independent states during the federal collapse, including Kaliningrad as the fourth Baltic Republic and Primorsky as a new Pacific state, both with prospects of economic integration with wealthier foreign neighbours.

Several other temporary state structures based on regional identity have existed in Russia, and some local activists may seek their revival or use them as historic precedent for claiming legitimate statehood. These include the Siberian Republic and the Far Eastern Republic, whose territorial span would encompass several *krais* and *oblasts.* During the post-Tsarist civil wars, Siberian regionalists – who claimed a distinct identity and sought to emulate the American War of Independence against Russian colonial rule – established a provisional government for an Autonomous Siberia in January 1918. However, the formation was eliminated by the Bolsheviks. Nonetheless, a significant sector of ethnic Russians may support the sovereignty or secession of regions in which they have ancestral roots and have few ties with Moscow, regardless of common language. A Republic of Siberia could be one of the first entities to proclaim its independence. The large Ukrainian population in the Far East may also seek greater regional autonomy and closer links with Ukraine. Descendants of Ukrainians and other nations, including Tatars and Chuvash, who were deported to southern Siberia and the Pacific territories, have undergone a process of cultural and linguistic rejuvenation since the Soviet decomposition.

Secession based on ethno-national principles could also spark internal disputes between majority and minority groups or with a Russian ethnic population seeking to remain within a single federation. Some republican leaders or movements supporting secession from Russia may also campaign for territorial acquisitions and the amalgamation of neighbouring regions containing ethnic kindred. As the fault lines widen, Putin or his successor can turn to Russian ethno-nationalism to try and maintain Kremlin control, prevent the secession of Russian-majority regions, and preserve a core Russian state.

The deliberate pursuit of ethnic divisions through violence would be reminiscent of the developments that occurred during a collapsing federal Yugoslavia during the 1990s. It is worth remembering the "Yugoslav scenario" was varied, with only limited military skirmishes in Slovenia, a small guerrilla war in Macedonia, a short NATO bombing campaign in Serbia, and no armed conflicts in Montenegro. In marked contrast, the wars in Croatia, Bosnia-Herzegovina, and Kosovo took the lives of tens of thousands of people and displaced millions more. Different parts of the Russian Federation could follow these diverse scenarios with outright war between the centre and some republics and regions. Moscow can emulate Serbia by mobilising ethnic Russians to carve out ethnically homogenous regions from rebellious republics. It can fund, arm, and direct militia groups and volunteer movements, as in Milošević's Yugoslavia, to kill and expel non-Russian populations. Various ethnonationalist revolutionary movements advocating violence against non-Russians could be recruited, and some have prior experience in violent attacks against ethnic minorities and political opponents. Returning fighters from Ukraine's Donbas and other conflict zones can gravitate toward internal territorial and ethnic battlegrounds.

In the midst of outright conflict with Moscow, the process of de-russification can intensify in some former federal subjects. New governments will seek to protect a burgeoning identity and independent statehood and seek to shield themselves against the "Russian World." In some cases, this could involve purging ethnic Russians from significant political positions, confiscating Russian-owned businesses, and even expelling Russian populations viewed as a potential fifth column. "Ethnic cleansing" operations could be conducted by the central government and by some republican regimes in order to ensure ethnic homogeneity or to seize territory and create larger states.

Russia could experience a number of civil wars, reminiscent of the period between 1917 and 1926 during the collapse of the Tsarist empire and following the Bolshevik seizure of power. Several of these previous conflicts were wars of national liberation to restore or establish states independent from the Russian empire. Such future struggles can include guerrilla wars against the central government or against regional governments loyal to Moscow. The Kremlin will find its security forces too thinly stretched to handle simultaneous liberation wars across the country and may only be able to maintain control over Moscow, Saint Petersburg, and the core *oblasts* of European Russia. A smaller Russia may not necessarily gravitate toward democracy and regional cooperation. It could evolve into an aggressive power. Nonetheless, its military capabilities would be significantly reduced, its geopolitical aspirations narrowed, and it would be focused on ensuring state survival rather than imperial expansion. In the midst of the escalating conflicts, competing factions with distinct ideologies or regional programmes could claim to be the legitimate national governments of a new Russian state. The country could then face a Libyan, Iraqi, or Syrian scenario with competing political forces fighting over disputed territories, economic resources, and political authority in a shrunken Russia.

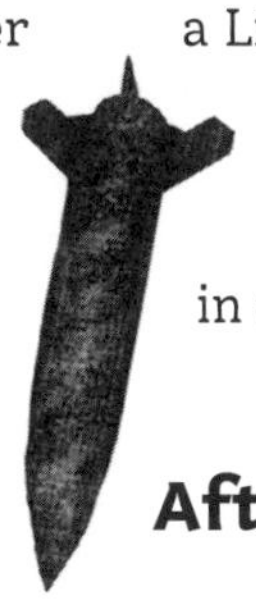

After the Rupture

Aspiring countries emerging from a truncated Russian Federation are unlikely to gain rapid international recognition. Some may evolve into "frozen states" with unresolved internal ethnic and territorial conflicts or even become embroiled in external disputes with neighbours. The process of fracture could lead to several destabilising scenarios, whether through spillovers of armed conflicts, refugee outflows, territorial wars, energy and trade disruptions, or various military incursions. However, it could also result in the creation of several viable states with a notable degree of political stability,

a sufficient economic base, a favourable geographic location, and governments committed to international cooperation.

Statehood is an important condition for the preservation and development of national identity. The proto-states and other entities which emerge from the Russian Federation will not be uniform in their internal political systems and administrative structures. Several could develop into embryonic democracies with newly formed political parties competing for office as the republican or regional institutions achieve independence. They will seek workable models of sovereignty and may look toward the three Baltic States (Estonia, Latvia, Lithuania), and other post-Soviet countries for assistance and guidance.

New autocrats may emerge in some former federal units, and a few may resemble mini-Russias, with corrupt authoritarian local leaders constructing personalistic fiefdoms through control of the legislature, law enforcement, and the judicial system, combined with internal repression and media censorship. They may also invent or exaggerate the extent of internal and external threats in order to pose as the staunch defenders of the integrity of the new state. Due to prolonged repression, there is limited organised democratic opposition who could challenge local autocrats in the majority of regions.

In parts of the North Caucasus, the traditional ethno-clanship system of self-government will gain strength and replace Moscow-appointed regional administrations. In some former autonomous republics, local leaders could construct ethnocratic states curtailing the rights of non-natives. Secession can also lead to intra-elite power struggles based on rival patronage networks within the fledgling states if stability and representative government cannot be ensured. Moves toward independence will become a test of strength for regional identity and multi-ethnic co-existence in a number of ethnically mixed territories. Some republics may witness ethnic discrimination, purges, expulsions, or the voluntary exodus of non-titular nationalities, as the new leaders seek to create more ethnically homogenous entities. Many nascent states will also face economic problems when Moscow's federal allocations are terminated. Moreover, business operations and foreign investments will be discouraged if there is persistent political uncertainty, social unrest, ethnic conflicts, official corruption, and organised criminality.

Nonetheless, several post-Russia statelets could become more democratically oriented, business friendly, and receptive to international investment, especially those bordering democratic or prosperous foreign states. They could also pursue broad ethnic representation in government institutions in order to provide key constituencies with a stake in the new state and support its independence. However, each developing country will confront the enormous task of reconstruction and economic stabilisation and will need significant international diplomatic and material support. Assistance is more likely to be forthcoming for fledgling states able to ensure a relatively stable and predictable political, social, and legal environment, or those possessing resources and industries which can attract foreign investment.

Disputes between some post-Russia states could escalate toward armed clashes in which the control of nuclear weapons, military equipment, energy infrastructure, or critical resources could become a major source of contention. However, it would be misleading to assume a fractured Russian state will generate conflict and chaos in all directions, as claimed by Kremlin propaganda. Developing states may follow the example of post-colonial Africa by maintaining the previous administrative boundaries in order to avoid persistent conflicts over territories and minorities, where virtually every state possesses some claim against neighbours. Such a solution may be pursued by the new governments regardless of whether the proto-states develop as democracies or autocracies.

The dismantling of Moscow's rule can also encourage the emergence of pan-regional and pan-republic associations. Such initiatives could evolve into federal or confederal state structures. A precursor of such a process was visible in the 1990s with the development of eight inter-regional associations spanning most of Russia that were subdued by Yeltsin. The most significant was the Siberian Agreement, based in Novosibirsk and including 19 regions with the objective of coordinating economic activities between western and eastern Siberia. Moscow resisted any moves toward forging agreements with a single Siberian unit, as it was fearful of fortifying an extensive pan-regional identity and encouraging Siberian separatism. The Urals Republic declared in 1993 could also become an inspiration for a new confederal arrangement between former *oblasts, krais,* and national republics.

In the Middle Volga region, the Idel-Ural State can be revived. This was a short-lived independent republic proclaimed in March 1918 in Tatarstan's capital Kazan and asserting the unification of Tatars, Bashkirs, Chuvash, and other nations and their liberation from the Russian empire. It included present-day Tatarstan, Bashkortostan, and Orenburg Oblast, with some activists even claiming part of the Caspian Sea coastline. A present-day incarnation of a Middle Volga union

promoted by the Free Idel-Ural movement would include the republics of Tatarstan, Bashkortostan, Chuvashia, Udmurtia, Mari-El, and Mordovia – the latter renamed as Erzyano-Moksha in recognition of the two constituent nations. The new Idel-Ural state is envisaged as a confederation in which each republic would maintain its own domestic and foreign policy. Some activists have proposed a larger confederation to include the Komi Republic, Perm Krai, and Orenburg Oblast to give the new state a foreign border with Kazakhstan.

Inter-republican initiatives can also include the revival of the independent Mountainous Republic of the Northern Caucasus that existed between 1918 and 1922. This confederal republic included seven constituent states: Dagestan, Chechnya, Ingushetia, Ossetia, Circassia, Abkhazia, and the Nogai steppes. During the Soviet collapse, attempts were made to revive the Mountainous Republic, and an Assembly of the Mountain Peoples of the North Caucasus was convened in August 1989 and renamed as the Confederation of the Mountain Peoples of the Caucasus. In October 1990, it was declared as a successor state to the Mountain Republic of 1918 and as separate from the Russian Federation. In November 1991, representatives from fourteen peoples of the North Caucasus signed a treaty formally founding the Confederation. It was not based on Islamic religious principles but on multi-ethnic solidarity and opposition to Russian imperialism and colonialism.

In northern Siberia, the republic of Sakha would become the largest state extracting itself from the Russian Federation with its own Arctic coastline, ports, and significant energy and mineral resources. With an astute political leadership, it could benefit from the expanding Northern Sea Route and significantly develop its trading potential with the Asia-Pacific region as well as with southern Siberia and China. Other northern regions along the Arctic Ocean may follow Sakha's example on the global stage, including the Komi Republic, the Nenets Autonomous Okrug, and the Yamalo-Nenets Autonomous Okrug.

A parallel development to republican independence would be the emergence of sovereign Russian majority regions, some of which federate or confederate to create new state structures. This would signal the emergence of an ethnic Russian national state, although its political composition and the prerogatives of the central government are likely to generate competition and even conflict between regional leaders and the administrations in Moscow and Saint Petersburg. The fracturing of the Russian Federation will also have an impact on all neighbouring countries. Some states will be vulnerable to spillovers of conflict or subject to Moscow's provocations designed to divert attention from its domestic upheaval. Other countries stand to benefit from Russia's weaknesses and cleavages by easing their security concerns, expanding their influence, and even regaining territories lost to various iterations of the Muscovite empire.

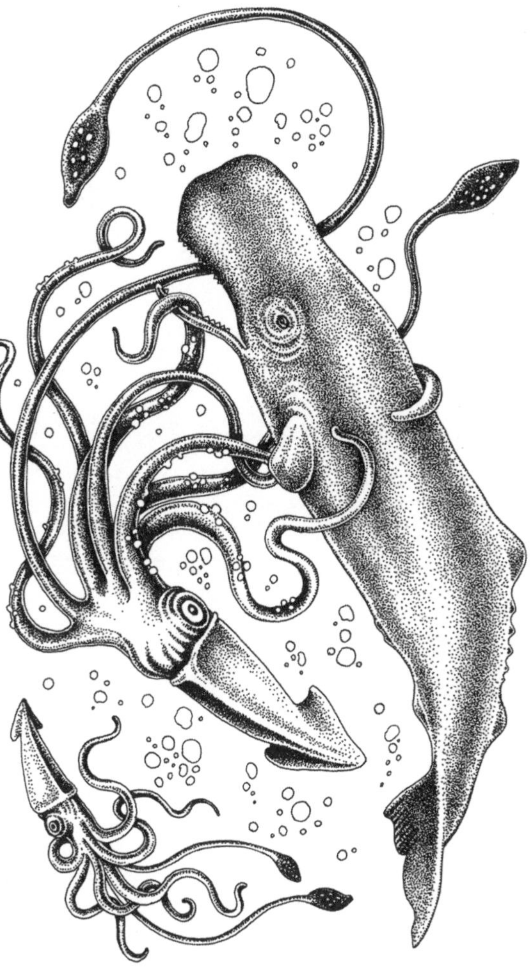

Deus ex Ucraina

Story by Oleksii Dubrov
Illustrated by Mykhailo Aleksandrov

I WOKE UP THAT DAY TO THE SOUND OF EXPLOSIONS AND THE WHISTLING of missiles as they flew by my window and crashed into the centre of Moscow. Instinctively, I threw aside the warm duvet and, dressed only in thin summer pajamas, dropped to the floor. It was inlaid with tiny, "old school" tiles, four of which could fit into the palm of my hand. The tiles typically decorated old stoves, but for some reason, in my apartment they were set into the floor. Each white tile was stamped with images of fanciful, impossibly shaped blue shells. Nature would never have created anything like those shells, I thought. It was highly unlikely the local artisan had ever seen real seashells.

There was no air-raid siren as the warning system had been ceremoniously dismantled 10 years before. Yet somehow, I knew what was happening and what had to be done. I think my knowing was connected to the epilepsy and strange sensation of déjà vu I have suffered since childhood.

My first experience with déjà vu happened when I was just 10. Back then, I was living in the Chinese Occupation Zone of Moscow. The director of the orphanage, old Mrs Mao, who, judging by her appearance, was way over a hundred years old, was once again taking a swing at me with her cane. She walked with it not because she was old, but because despite her hundred-plus years, she was bizarrely still a very obese woman. For the life of me, I don't remember why she was swinging her cane at me at the time. I was a good student. And, apparently, I wasn't being singled out for bad behaviour. But something would come over her from time to time, and she would randomly take a swing. What was it called officially? Oh yeah. Demonstrating a "teaching moment." Honestly, I would simply call it a beating given to anyone who wound up nearby when she was red-hot with rage. More often than not, I was the one nearby. The Chinese children were almost never the target of her random swings.

So, I was 10-years-old, and one fine summer morning, while the smell of scrambled eggs left over from breakfast smeared on a classmate's clothing still hung in the air, Mrs Mao decided to demonstrate her "teaching moment" on me. Her cane had whistled through the air as she raised it over my head, when suddenly her swing stopped mid-stroke. The old woman cried out and froze in place with her arm above her head and her mouth wide open. She stood there for a few seconds, unmoving, like a stone statue, before crashing onto my desk with such force that it collapsed under her weight. The loud clattering made me flinch, and I realized I had dropped to the floor, right next to Mrs Mao, who had landed there a second or two earlier.

That should have been the happiest day of my childhood because the evil boarding school director Mrs Mao never again raised a hand to hurt me. However, it was also the day when my first epileptic seizure happened. Or so they tell me, because I don't remember it too clearly. All I recall is the desk shrieking as it shattered, hitting the wooden floor, smashed to smithereens from Mrs Mao's weight, and the shrieking sound causing me to dive to the floor instinctively, wrapping my hands around my head. I felt a hurricane ripping my stomach apart and every possible colour flashing before my eyes as my body began to shake violently. Honestly, I can't say I was particularly frightened by the whole thing. Subsequent events sometimes emerge as random scenes in my dreams: the appointment at the doctor's office, after which I was told to always take some kind of pills; photographs of Mrs Mao's funeral, which I saw on the boarding school's

website. Since then, I've had a recurring dream where a beautiful woman in a military uniform is beckoning to me. I've never been able to follow her, no matter how hard I've tried.

It's said people who suffer from epilepsy experience déjà vu several times more frequently than individuals who do not. Déjà vu is a state when two realities exist inside of you: you are physically in one place, while all your sensory organs and your subconscious are somewhere far away. The latter reality may be connected to your memories, to something which actually happened. But sometimes you have a completely foreign experience. You sense the situation is somewhat familiar, but the chances of recalling any details are practically zero. It feels like gazing into a mirror of the past, but the reflection is maximally blurred.

After that day at age 10, almost every instance of loud clattering or shrieking I have experienced has triggered my stupid déjà vu, which is inevitably followed by an epileptic seizure. Despite being unusually forgetful and inattentive, I developed a habit of keeping the pills in the pocket of my trousers to prevent the onset of a seizure. But the pills don't stop the déjà vu, the gurgling in my stomach, or the flashing lights in my eyes. On the contrary, they tend to prolong the symptoms. Manifestations of the déjà vu last up to 10 minutes, and until they pass, I am unable to force my brain and body to function normally. For some time afterwards, my emotions seem to disappear altogether.

Those were the sensations I experienced that day on the floor of my Moscow apartment. Except now I was no longer in the Chinese zone. I was living in the zone controlled by the United Nations. That day, the missiles flew into our occupation zone from beyond the Urals, where international organisations were implementing a project to re-educate the Russians.

I had also been working on the same project for a few years now, as a janitor. They paid good money and provided me with a sunny, stylish, futuristic-looking apartment. The windows, which I always kept closed and covered with rolling shutters, faced the former Red Square, where out of all the old buildings, only the mausoleum remained. It was empty now, because during last week's terrorist attack, the body was stolen. And the square was no longer red since city planners from Berlin had covered it with grey concrete. The apartment didn't really appeal to me, particularly the layout, but my employer was paying a crazy amount of money for the rent. How could I object? I never considered myself overworked, but somehow, I always felt exhausted and broken.

The day of the attack had promised to be sunny and warm, the first such day in the summer of 2049. Forecasters, however, failed to predict precipitation in the form of bombs, with their high-pitched penetrating whistle and thunderous blasts as they fell to the ground and exploded. The situation seemed oddly familiar, though I had grown accustomed to distrust my memory. One day I would forget the keys to the apartment, another day my watch. Sometimes I would heat up a frozen pizza and forget it in the oven until the smoke detector reminded me about it. In her day, old Mrs Mao forced me to write everything down. She even taught me how to write by hand, even though no one had been doing that for a long time already. After she died, I joined the rest of the world and also stopped writing by hand.

As soon as my windows began to rattle, I felt a chill envelop my internal organs, penetrating deep into my bones. My mouth dried up. I automatically popped an anti-seizure pill into my mouth and swallowed it with the help of what little saliva I had, then dropped to the floor. Adding insult to injury, the X-shaped tattoo on my right hand started to itch fiercely. My scratching aggravated the chronic infection, turning my skin red and slightly swollen.

I couldn't immediately comprehend what had just happened. Of course, I understood these were combat operations, but who could be attacking? At first, I thought it was the Chinese, since their zone of occupation in Moscow, and what was formerly Russia, was the largest. No one really trusted them. The Chinese are always smiling, except Mrs Mao, of course. She never smiled. That's probably why some children admired her – for her lack of insincerity. No one trusts a smile anymore, especially a Chinese one.

After an hour, the first series of explosions subsided. I listened to the constant wail of sirens emitted from ambulances and firefighting drones. I stayed on the floor for another 15 minutes, then got up and moved to look out the window. The cloudless blue sky was daubed with billowing plumes of thick, black smoke. The streets were flooded with vehicles of every sort: hovercrafts, aerial police drones, and delivery drones loaded with suitcases. Driverless cars were stuck in an endless traffic jam. Police drones usually handled this kind of Babylonian pandemonium, but it looked as if their software had crashed; the machines were stuck, fluttering in the air. A swarm of pedestrians moved along the sidewalk, dragging heavy bags and sleeping children. My mind urged me to follow the crowd, but after my epileptic seizure I was powerless to decide.

Only then did it occur to me to check the news on my watch. I went to the nightstand and picked up the device. The Chinese watch was old but had been working well for two years now. The miniature, round watch face could project a holographic image measuring ten by fifteen centimetres, which was good enough for my needs. I pressed the watch face, but nothing happened. I pressed it a second time and again, nothing. *"Damn it! I forgot to charge the watch overnight!"* I thought. I couldn't charge it then since the power was out in my apartment. The bombs had likely damaged the nearest wind turbine on a roof a few blocks from my place.

I decided I'd ask the people on the street where they were headed and simply follow them. I put some things into my backpack (water, underwear, and my favourite poster of London's Gherkin skyscraper on 30 St Mary Axe). Then it hit me: I should stop by work, even though it was my day off. The office of the NGO "New Russians," where I worked as a janitor, was in a business centre in another neighbourhood. Maybe they had power there. I decided it was better to charge my device before leaving town as all my documents were on it. Visiting my neighbours to see if they had power didn't occur to me; even after five years of living here, I wasn't acquainted with any of them. And why would anyone help me anyway?

In the past, my blank disposition, which typically followed an epileptic seizure, had never attracted anyone's attention on the street. After all, everyone generally wore a similar expression. Right then, however, my calm composure appeared in stark contrast to the panic-stricken men and women overburdened by heavy suitcases, dumbfounded children, and terrified pets. Finally, after pushing my way through the chaotic crowds of people who continued running in all directions shouting "Achtung!" and "Cours plus vite!", I reached my office, where the only person I encountered was my boss, Günther Dupré. His coal-black hair, usually greased flat and neat with litres of styling gel, was dishevelled, sticking out all over the place.

"Hector, why did you haul your ass over here?" He stared at me through eyes skittish with fear.

This was the first time I heard this educated intellectual from the Saar utter the words "haul your ass."

"There's no electricity in my building, and my watch is dead. And where else should I go?" I held my hands out, palms up, in a shrug.

I have no relatives, and things have not worked out with friends. No, I'm not complaining about my colleagues, they were always nice to me. We often ate lunch together and socialised in the corridors. But as soon as we crossed the invisible border around our office, we became strangers. I was never invited to evening get-togethers in bars or for birthdays, so it wasn't surprising no one was curious about what happened to me today.

Günther was feverishly tapping on his work holographic screen, muttering under his breath in an aggressive tone and incessantly surveying his surroundings. I don't recall ever seeing him so frightened. Always demonstratively polite and friendly and dressed in a perfectly ironed shirt, he now resembled a timid fawn anticipating a tiger attack. I set my watch on the quick charge stand; a few minutes was sufficient for my model.

"Aren't you at all afraid about the bombs? You do realise our zone is completely defenceless?" Günther questioned me, without taking his eyes off the holo-screen. I remember noticing beads of heavy sweat on his face – another first.

"They told us war is impossible here," I replied, turning on my watch. "You think it's the Chinese?"

"Why didn't anyone warn me?" He sighed, covering his face with his hand. "After everything I've done!" At that moment Günther's holographic screen pinged. He flinched, then removed a round memory card no larger than his delicate pinkie fingernail from the device. Günther jumped to his feet and spoke to me with a distinct tremor in his voice.

"Ri-Right now it-it's st-still possible to be-be evacuated," he stammered, gazing through the window at the smoke rising on the horizon. He inhaled and exhaled a few times to gain some self-composure. "Come with me, n-now that you're here. It will probably be easier with the two of us."

"Evacuated where?" I asked.

"To P-P-Paris," he forced out, squeezing past between me and the table. Then he turned to me and said, "OK, I know you never smile, but could you at least be scared right now!?"

I shrugged and shuffled after him silently. By the time we dashed into the street, the effects of the morning's epileptic seizure had begun to fade, and once again my brain launched some non-autonomic processes. Trailing after Günther through a crowd of crazed eyes and gaping mouths, I looked at the plumes of smoke blanketing the sky in a dense dome. Smoke was settling near the ground as well, making it harder and harder to breathe. My throat became parched. People all around were coughing non-stop, like heavy smokers before they die.

Günther was right. Our part of Moscow was completely defenceless against any attack. All troops and equipment had been withdrawn from here when Mrs Mao was still alive, and that was 20 years ago. Back then, people said international organisations had achieved perpetual peace in this territory. In the Chinese occupation zone in the Far East, and the Baltic zone containing Saint Petersburg, garrisons had been reduced, but never fully withdrawn. The Ukrainians, on the other hand, increased their military presence in Smolensk and Moscow, for which they had been mercilessly criticised for the past two decades. Maybe it was the Ukrainians who had attacked. Where would the Russians in Zone 5 get missiles? True, for several months now, the "perpetual peace" in our zone had been breached by terrorist acts, for which none of the known organisations had taken responsibility. The UN was helpless.

Günther began panicking when a new round of bombings began. Swallowing a pill, I instantly fell to the ground. He stared at me for a few seconds, then dropped onto the ground following my lead.

“We have to get down into a shelter, to the subway station,” I proposed. Günther only gnawed his well-groomed fingernails. “The closest one...” I looked around, trying with all my might to stop my brain from falling into a post-epileptic stupor, “...is Dostoyevsky Square.”

“N-n-no!” Günther shrieked. “We’re close by, and the buses are only a few blocks away!”

Like the giant pulling Jack off the beanstalk, I grabbed Günther by his shirt collar and dragged him in the direction of the underpass. He was babbling incoherently and waving his arms, but to no avail. Tripping on the stairs a dozen times, he acquiesced in the end, backed away from me, and agreed to go down to the station.

Within seconds we found ourselves in a throng of frightened people of every nationality: Germans, the French, Poles, Serbs, Bulgarians, Lithuanians, and others. Many of them gawped suspiciously at my serene face; upon seeing it, they quickly turned away and tried to move as far as possible from me. Just like they always do.

We couldn't move far along the actual platform. After descending the awkward stairs of the out-of-service escalator, the crowd came to a standstill. I peered over the heads of the jostling people, who were continuously turning their heads to look in different directions, and spied a small cubbyhole in the wall, above which hung a red box with a fire hose.

Pushing through the throng, stepping on the feet of oncoming old ladies and dragging Günther Dupré behind me, I reached the spot. I was lucky. The floor under the fire hose turned out to be unoccupied and, bending down, we crawled inside and sat down. My tattoo started to itch again, and I tried to scratch it without anyone noticing, but failed. An old lady standing nearby shook her head reproachfully. I gestured to signal that there was enough space next to me for her to sit down, too. She pursed her lips in contempt at my offer.

I looked at Günther and saw he was clutching his knees, although this did not stop them from trembling. Waving my hand in front of his face, I forced him to turn his head to me, before assuring him, "The bombs won't reach us here."

He looked away. The crowd was humming. People were trying to activate the holographic screens on their telephones to learn the latest news. *"Yes! I can check, too!"* I thought and raised my left hand, but my watch wasn't there. I patted my trouser pockets, checked them again, but they were empty. *"Damn it,"* I thought. *"Did I forget the watch at the office right after charging it!?"* I jerked my head back and slammed it hard against the granite wall. I was overcome with pain, forcing me to clench my teeth. Feverishly rubbing the back of my head, I asked Dupré, "Günther, can you give me your watch? I'll try to find some news."

"There were rumours going around the office you're from Ukraine. Is that right?" he asked, extending his device to me.

"I'm an orphan," I replied, pressing the watch face. But the holographic screen was blank, and eventually a small icon appeared, announcing "No connection." I returned the watch to him. "My mother supposedly fled from Ukraine during the war of 2022. I think my father was killed. Then, after the victory, some international programme packed me off to a Chinese orphanage in Moscow. That's all I know."

"In other words, you don't have anyone?" he asked in surprise.

I shook my head.

"My wife and daughter are in Paris," Günther smiled. "They're working in the family business, a bookstore."

"Aha," was all I could utter. I suspected in this situation I was required to say something more, but small talk had never been my forte. Especially since no one had ever discussed personal matters with me; it had only ever been work-related stuff such as "It's dirty over here" or "Clean over there." The most I ever heard was, "Oh, you got a haircut" and "What cool new sneakers." An awkward silence fell upon us. It seemed to me I was the one who was supposed to break it.

"Ah, so, what do you think?" I began. "Did the Chinese or the Ukrainians attack? The Ukrainians probably did not like our programme to re-educate the Russians."

Günther opened his mouth to say something when, suddenly, the people around us began to move. I got up. Everyone was heading for the escalator.

"It looks like things have quieted down," I said to Günther, and we joined the throng. Going up a stationary escalator was much harder than going down. One saving grace was that the flow of people stopped frequently, giving everyone a chance to catch their breath.

Once we reached the exit from the subway into the underpass, I noticed something was wrong. We had been intermittently stopping all the time because there were people holding weapons stationed at the top of the stairs. I had no doubt they were the attackers. After all, our zone was demilitarised a long time ago. They did not resemble the Chinese or Ukrainian armies because they were all dressed differently, a hodgepodge of clothing, and they were not carrying standardised equipment.

"They are not Chinese. Or Ukrainians," I whispered to Günther, who, it seemed, had become even more frightened.

"B-b-because they are R-r-russians," he replied.

"How do you know? And where did they get their weapons?" It was stupid of me to have said this out loud because I attracted the attention of the soldiers – or, more accurately, the armed individuals, whoever they were – and they started watching me. I tried to lower my head, but still it stuck out above the crowd.

"Show me your documents," one of them said in Russian. Yes, he was definitely Russian. Even though it was summer, he was wearing a worn-out black sweater, pocked with holes, and heavy faded jeans. His face was hidden by a homemade balaclava, which looked to me like a huge, knitted sock with eyeholes cut out sloppily and unevenly. One of the holes was big and open all the way to his brow, the other was a slit, so thin you couldn't even see his eyelashes.

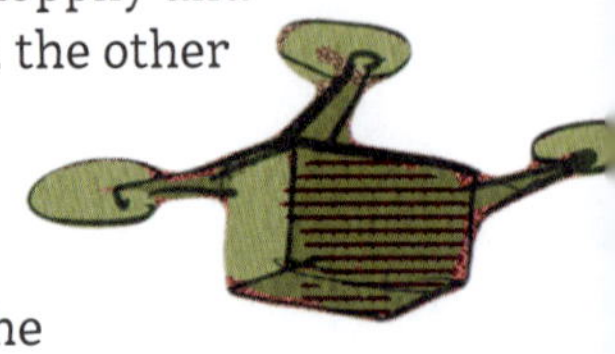

Günther Dupré, his head bowed, proffered his French passport with a quivering hand (they still issued paper passports). But the man who was supposed to be inspecting it didn't even glance at the document. Instead, he looked directly at me.

"Mine is digital," I shrugged, "But I lost my watch..."

"What are you babbling about? Speak Russian!" the armed man shouted at me.

"An electronic passport," I repeated and pointed to Dupré's watch then to my bare wrist. He must have misunderstood me because he tore the watch off Dupré's wrist and put it in his pocket. Günther Dupré looked at me angrily. The armed man called out to another and said loudly, "Take them to Nikolskaya!"

"What for? And where is Nikolskaya now?" asked another armed man, spinning the old paper map round and round as if it was on a steering wheel, before pivoting his head left to right to look around the street.

During my five years of working for the non-governmental organisation, I had found it strange that Russians beyond the Urals did not believe their fathers or grandfathers blew up Moscow in the fall of 2023, and so today the streets were totally different. They were all redesigned and renamed in honour of Russian cultural figures and literary personalities of the past. Where Nikolskaya Street used to be was now the intersection of Brodsky Street and Nieznayka Lane. International organisations spent billions of euros on re-education programs to inform Russians about their history. But why were these armed men with paper maps still not familiar with their past, so many years later, in the year 2049?

I opened my mouth to give directions, but Günther interrupted, pointing in the direction of the promised evacuation.

"N-n-nikolskaya is th-th-there," he stammered, pointing to the left, to the only part of the horizon still not covered with the black smoke from the fires.

We walked slowly, tripping over rocks and debris. As we passed a large building in flames that were slowly dying out, I smelled a distinct metallic odour. As soon as it reached my nose, my whole body was racked with horror, and I was struck with déjà vu. Except this time, I saw a different place in front of my eyes, one similarly burned but definitely not Moscow. The image quickly disappeared and reappeared several times, like individual scenes an editor had forgotten to cut from the final version of a film. The destroyed city flashing before me was next to a sea. But it didn't smell like water at all; instead, it had the same odour I had just noticed, that of a recent fire.

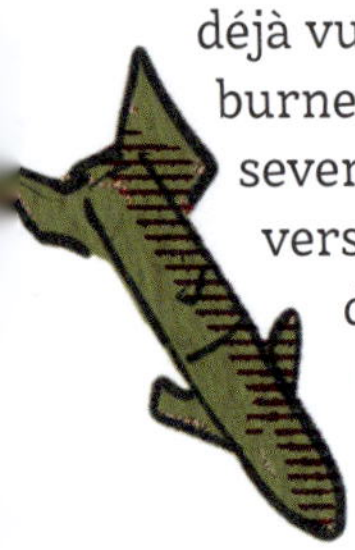

A blow from the butt of a machine gun promptly knocked these images out of my mind. The man holding the weapon was clearly aiming for my temple, but he missed a little and only grazed the back of my head. I staggered and couldn't maintain my balance from the surprise smack, falling on all fours. I leaned my weight on my hands, straightened my elbows, and pushed myself back up to find my footing.

We turned the corner and stopped at Ostap Bender Square. It's a quaint spot surrounded by high-rises, with about a dozen trees in the centre of the square, now crisp and charred with a few flames still lapping their trunks. On the balcony of one of the buildings hung a bed sheet with the words "For Peace" painted in black letters. *"Well, at least it covered a bit of the ridiculously decorated façade,"* I thought. My attention was caught by a group of people walking away from the entrance. Each one of the men was carrying a toilet, some of which still had floor tiles hanging from their bases where they had been ripped out. Machine guns were in a heap next to the door. I remember Dupré saying at a meeting we had purchased millions of toilets for the Russians. *"Damn,"* I thought, *"Do they still need them?"*

"So, why did we come here?" asked one of our guards, gesturing at the building. The other simply shrugged. He glared at the men with the toilets and shouted, "Look at them cashing in at our expense!"

I glanced at Günther Dupré, who was looking from side to side in what was, for this day, his usual state of panic.

"The transport should have been here," he whispered to me.

"Well, perhaps delivery drones," I said ironically, referring to the small size of Ostap Bender Square. "I think you've made a mistake about any kind of evacuation from here."

I didn't think Dupré's face could get any paler. At this point, it looked as if the hair on his head was turning grey in real time. He took a few cautious steps toward me and shoved his hand into my pocket.

"What are you doing?" I said, jumping back, almost bumping the shoulder of one of the guards. It appeared the guard was trying to contact his commander on some ancient looking device, a black, rectangular box with buttons and a stick-like antenna on the top. The device made an awful hissing sound. One time I saw Mrs Mao using something similar because she flatly refused to buy a watch.

Taking advantage of the chaotic situation, Günther Dupré took a few steps to the side. I tried to catch hold of him to stop him, but he was too far away already. He took a few more quiet steps away from the guards, creeping up to the closest building. He stopped directly beneath the sheet proclaiming "For Peace." Suddenly, our escort, the one holding the communication device from which a voice was yelling, turned and conveyed a command to the other guard, "We have orders to liquidate these two." The men raised their weapons, preparing to fire.

Seeing Günther had moved, one of them shouted, "Halt!" and began shooting in Günther's direction.

Shocked by the sound of gunfire, the men in the distance dropped several toilets, which smashed into pieces beneath them. I dropped to the sidewalk and swallowed my last pill. Out of the corner of my eye, I saw Günther veering sharply from side to side and running toward the entrance of the building. The bullets finally caught up with him, and he fell to the ground. The commander of the toilet-carrying-detachment was yelling at his subordinates who had dropped their precious cargo. My two guards quickly ran to the still-warm Dupré and began rummaging through his pockets.

I raised my head and looked around. The toilet movers were continuing their procession, while my guards were swearing, unsuccessful in their search of Günther's pockets. Then they looked up at me and yelled, "He must have the flash drive!"

"Flash drive?" I thought, *"What are they talking about?"* Then I remembered Günther had shoved something in my pocket. I started rummaging through my pockets, but my hands were so sweaty, I couldn't feel anything. The epilepsy medication had slowed down my ability to think, and only after the first bullet flew over my head and hit a tree did I to decide to make a run for it. Splinters from the bullet-ridden

tree, mingling with the flashes in my eyes, flew in every direction. I was bent over when the second bullet hit me in the leg. My body stiffened and a dull pain suffused my muscles, but the adrenalin was blunting my senses.

Mustering all my willpower, I managed to jerk my body into motion and miraculously ended up behind a tree. *"I'm alive,"* I thought. More shots rang out. I clamped my eyes shut and saw multi-coloured lights flashing and twirling in a kind of chaotic dance. My head began to ache, and I grasped it in my hands, squeezing with all my might, as if that would stop the pain. Writhing in agony from the headache, I totally forgot about my wounded leg. My ears became plugged from the next bullet whistling past me. Suddenly, the kaleidoscope in front of my eyes ceased, and all at once, I was enveloped in complete silence and darkness.

I don't know whether I lost consciousness or if my medication failed and I succumbed to another seizure. But I came to when someone forced me to stand and pushed my back against a tree.

"Who are you?" a menacing voice demanded. He repeated the question. He wasn't speaking Russian, but I understood him. *"Is he speaking Ukrainian?"* flashed through my mind.

"Hector Kharabetts, I live here...I'm a civilian," I managed to squeeze out the words just barely peeking through my clenched eyelids.

"Do you know Günther Dupré?" The man in a military uniform was shorter than I am, but he still managed to loom over me.

"Y-yes, I worked for him," I said.

“Well, then say your good-byes.” The man abruptly took a few steps back and aimed his weapon at my chest. He was just about to pull the trigger when another voice interrupted him.

“Wait!” The new voice was higher-pitched but scratchy, like that of a smoker. A woman in full military gear appeared in front of me. I had a feeling I had seen her somewhere before; however, my memory refused to function normally. The woman patted me down, rooting through my pockets. While checking the last one, she removed a small memory card, which I recognised from that morning in Günther's office, and which it appears he later shoved into my pocket. It was so small I had missed it when searching myself.

"We'll talk to him first," the woman said in English.

"But Colonel, Ma'am, he was aiding the enemy," replied the man who had just been preparing to shoot me, a disappointed tone in his voice. The woman waved him away, indicating the order was not open to debate.

From this point, everything happened at lightning-fast speed, yet I remember each detail vividly. I managed to catch a glimpse of the dead bodies of the guards and their colleagues with the toilets while I was being led around the corner to Sharikov Street. There, I was shoved into a helicopter. A few minutes later, we were in the Ukrainian Occupation Zone of Moscow.

The helicopter landed on a roof, and I was hustled swiftly into the building. There was no time to even glance around. Moments later, I was sitting with my hands bound, in a small room with glass walls, positioned at a table on which a tablet and a file of papers were laid out. Opposite me sat the woman responsible for the fact I was still alive, and near the door stood a soldier in full uniform with a machine gun and a blue-and-yellow chevron on his sleeve. I knew a lot about Chinese people and Europeans, but I had no idea what to expect from those who were likely of the same blood as me. The woman remained silent until the doctor, who had entered the room and rebandaged my wounded leg had left.

"Do you speak Ukrainian?" The female colonel asked me in Ukrainian.

"I understand a little, but I speak better in Chinese or English," I managed to say, looking down at the floor.

"Good," the woman continued, in English. "You were an accomplice of Günther Dupré?"

"An accomplice?" I repeated, confused.

"For years, you supplied weapons to the Russians, and now you have the result." The colonel took out a pack of chewing gum and tossed two pieces into her mouth. I looked up, directing my gaze towards her. She was chewing slowly and observing me carefully.

"What weapons?!" I was outraged and, for the first time in my life, nearly raised my voice. "We provided educational programmes, teaching, and support. There weren't any weapons!"

I don't know what my face was communicating, but she smiled. Maybe she didn't believe me. All of a sudden, she jumped up, leaned over the table, and yelled right in my face, "For five years, pursuing your good intentions, you put money right into the hands of those idiots! Didn't it occur to you they would spend it on something else? Acts of terrorism were taking place almost every week!"

I think that was the moment I recognised her. For years, I had seen her, but was unable to get near her. She was the same woman who was calling to me in my dreams. I suspect I looked like a fool. Here I was, being accused of a crime, with a broad grin on my face and a relieved expression. The colonel frowned. Then she heard something through her earpiece, sat back down, and picked up her tablet, studying something on the screen. Gradually, the contours of her face began to soften.

"So, Mr. Hector Khara-d-m-bts..." The colonel stumbled over my surname, without stopping her energetic gum-chewing. She was beautiful, just like the woman in my dreams. But why on earth would I think she was the woman in my dreams? The tattoo on my hand started to itch again, and I tried to scratch it with the edge of the plastic binders strapped around my wrists.

The colonel noticed what I was doing and stared at my hand. After a few more chews, she removed the gum from her mouth and stuck it under the table.

"Why didn't you say this was your first mandatory job placement after the orphanage? And that you were working there as a janitor?"

"Is that important?" I shrugged.

"Yes, it is." The woman clasped her hands and leant on them against the table. "A Ukrainian child from Mariupol, who in 2022 was forcibly taken away from his mother." Her lips trembled slightly. "My father was killed while taking my grandmother and us to Zaporizhzhia." She extended her arm and raised the sleeve of her uniform for a split second, showing me the X-shaped tattoo just below her wrist, a mirror of my own tattoo. She began shuffling through the papers in the folder, as if she was afraid the guard at the door would notice the tattoo. "After that, you were sent to the orphanage and a job you couldn't refuse," she continued. "You even safeguarded data about the black ledger and illegal financing of the 'New Russians,' which will now untie our hands."

The colonel said something into her communicator, stood, and began pacing. At first, she circled the room a few times in silence. Then I sensed she was standing behind me. I'm willing to bet she was trying to peer into my consciousness to figure out if my intentions were evil. After a few moments she continued her pacing and asked, "So, you really believed you could re-educate them?"

"At the general meeting, Dupré reported consultations were held with psychologists, human rights defenders, social democrats, the UN... And everyone supported the project," I said. "The Russians once had a great culture but suffered from tyranny, so we decided to show them a different path. A controlled experiment, so to speak. The idea was *(I had read it on a website several times to commit it to memory):* We trust them, we help them to feel like fully-fledged people, we cooperate with them, we enable each one's personal growth..."

"Hah!" She interrupted with disdain. Just then, someone waved to the colonel through the glass, and she left the room.

After she shut the glass door, I saw her explaining something to someone at length, subtly gesturing with her hands. She listened to the reply for a long time without moving. I barely spoke Ukrainian and was unable to lipread a single word. Suddenly, a broad smile appeared on her face, and she embraced the man she was speaking with. It was the first time in my life a smile seemed sincere to me. Without thinking, I smiled as well.

Her conversation completed, she opened the glass door and said, "After everything is over, you can return to China."

"Over?" I asked, but she had already left.

I remained seated. Half an hour later, someone walked in and whispered something into the guard's ear, and he ordered me to stand up. After removing the plastic ties binding my hands, he brought me to a small but cosy room with a bed, dresser, table, and chair, and a separate bathroom with a shower. The whole time I was being interrogated, I thought they'd put me in jail, but I lucked out, ending up in a warm room with a soft mattress.

After taking a hot shower and lying down to try and get to sleep, I heard more explosions through the window I had opened to air out the room. My hand reached automatically for the epilepsy pills in the pocket of my trousers hanging on the back of a chair, but the pocket was empty. My breathing quickened and I started hyperventilating. It felt like ants were crawling over my body. Something stirred in my stomach.

But this... this was different somehow. A few minutes passed, and there was no seizure. And no déjà vu. When my mind came to this realisation, I did not drop to the floor, as I had done in the past. I stayed in place, in the warm bed, without pills, but with the sound of explosions in the background. This time, the once-menacing noises of bombardment acted like a lullaby. After a few seconds, my eyes closed, exhaustion overcame me, and I fell into a deep, calm sleep.

"Zone 5 no longer exists," the colonel jubilantly informed me the next morning, when I answered the knock on the door to my room. "The information from your organisation's flash drive has shocked everyone in Europe, especially those at the top," she said, pointing at the ceiling.

I rubbed my eyes, trying to understand where I was and what was happening. My leg started aching from yesterday's injury, and I winced.

"I spoke with the director," she smiled. "He's going to allow you to stay in Ukraine, if you'd like. According to law, they can even issue you a passport if you find some information about your relatives. Or you can head for China, to be among the people you grew up with. What do you want to do?"

"This is all so unexpected," I mumbled, sitting down on the bed. The woman stared straight into my eyes, which made me feel embarrassed. Then I thought about Mrs Mao, my work as a janitor in Moscow, and I burst out, "I don't want to go back there!"

"Good," the colonel said, smiling, and she patted me on my shoulder. She took out a small blue and white tube of cream and placed it in my hands. "This will stop the itching," she whispered, nodding to the tattoo, and left.

Still not fully awake, I forgot to ask her what happened to Zone 5. Raucous celebrations took place over the next few days, but no one could give me a concrete explanation. Everyone was chanting, "ROZ-YII-BAH-LY!" Some people said Zone 5 would now be a wasteland, while others said it was a giant toxic lake.

There was also no consensus on the fate of the local population. Ukrainian journalists claimed everyone there was killed or had "self-liquidated." Western experts insisted a group of people remained and had created a new religion – a cult worshipping the White Toilet. An Italian journalist even located a building not far from Kyiv from which, he believed, the Russians had stolen the artefact venerated by the cult during the war of 2022. But I think even if anyone survived, they would rather have worshipped the corpse from the mausoleum on Red Square; why else would the terrorists want to steal it? Incidentally, after Zone 5 disappeared, not a single act of terrorism took place anywhere in the world; few people noticed, but I sure did. The United Nations vanished just as imperceptibly.

At first, they put me up in a dormitory on the left bank of Kyiv and gave me a small stipend. I couldn't find a job, so in my spare time (and I had a lot of it), I studied Ukrainian. When I wasn't attending the Ukrainian language courses, I would visit the archives. After two weeks of searching, I found a record of my father. He was killed by Russian shelling in September 2022 during the liberation of Amvrosiivka. A staff member of the archives helped me to upload the document to a special database. A few weeks later, the repatriation service called me, issued me a passport, and offered to help me move back to the city where I was born: Mariupol.

The small house I live in is actually in a suburb of Mariupol, in a large cottage community called "Steel" on the shores of the Azov Sea. A general whose surname I don't remember gave me the keys and told me he was my father's brother-in-arms. The good news is, since I started living here beside the sea, my epileptic seizures have stopped, as has the sickening feeling of déjà vu. I no longer have problems with my memory. Now I even doubt I had the disease in the first place.

Sometimes when I'm daydreaming, I catch myself wanting to go back to Moscow and find out what is happening in Zone 5. But then I stroll along the seashore at dawn, my face catching the first timid sun rays and droplets of saltwater carried on the morning breeze, and I am convinced I should stay put. Besides bombs and déjà vu, there is nothing for me there. Not even the White Toilet everybody worships. Here, by the sea, beautiful seashells are scattered in the sand under my feet. And they're real.

I often think about the colonel and her smile – the first sincere smile I ever saw. I even looked her up on social media once and wrote to her, but I never got a reply. About 10 or 15 years later, I saw her being interviewed, and she was already a general. There on her face was the same smile that had made me smile.

I'm here, in Mariupol, on the shores of the Azov Sea. I no longer feel the need to close windows with roller shutters, but instead wake up every morning full of energy for my studies in architecture – my new profession. It keeps me busy. And, over time, I've even learned to forget about Mrs Mao and Günther Dupré, and that once, a long time ago, there existed a place known as Zone 5.

THE BLACK SEA WHALE CONTRIBUTORS

Marichka Melnyk (pen name): Marichka is adept at inviting her readers to become an integral part of the story she is telling, as if they are involved in the action alongside the characters, rather than remaining bystanders, watching the story unfold from afar. The experience is always thought-provoking: she delves into complex themes which may be shocking at times, but nevertheless are begging to be explored.

Viktoriia Antonenko: Often reading straight through the night, when asked what she wanted to be when she grew up, Viktoriia would answer "a librarian." In the end, though, she expanded on her dream job, and began to study the story form to craft her own creations. After completing her doctorate in historical studies, Viktoriia took on a new challenge as the Executive Editor of the Ukrainian language journal The Arc. Her stories elicit the deepest of emotions from readers. She was born and grew up in a "bandit's" village and categorically refuses to move anywhere else.

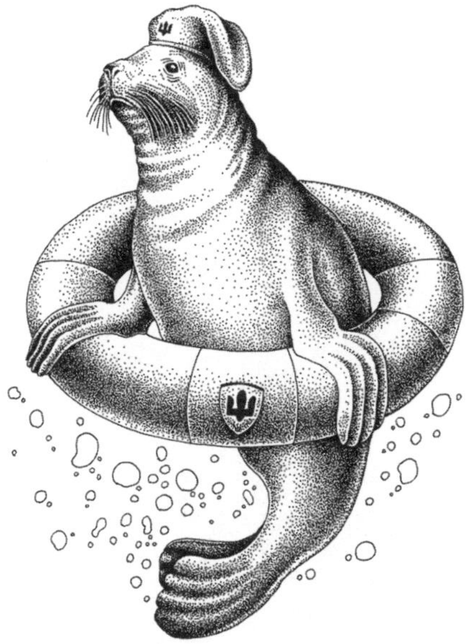

Mary Mycio (1959–2022) is the author of *Wormwood Forest: A Natural History of Chernobyl* (2005). Her writing has appeared in the *Los Angeles Times, Natural History, Newsday, Salon, Slate, Politico* and *Tablet*. She specialised in freedom of expression during war in her work as a lawyer.
We will always miss Mary.

Sergej Sumlenny is a German political analyst, founder of the European Resilience Initiative Centre in Berlin, and former Director at the Heinrich Böll Foundation Bureau in Kyiv (2015–2021). He prides himself on being a "recovering" Russian.

THE BLACK SEA WHALE CONTRIBUTORS

Oleksii Dubrov is a historian and recipient of the prestigious Gaude Polonia scholarship program in 2019. He has over eight years of experience working in the field of culture, and seventeen years of experience living in one of Ukraine's toughest cities, Kryviy Rih. A student of the humanities who loves numbers and statistics, Oleksii has been known to occasionally go over to the Dark Side (they have tasty cookies). He is currently serving in the Armed Forces of Ukraine.

Janusz Bugajski is a Senior Fellow at the Jamestown Foundation in Washington DC. His new book *Failed State: A Guide to Russia's Rupture* was published by Jamestown in July 2022. The Ukrainian translation is available from Arc.UA at *failedstate.com.ua.* He has authored 21 books and numerous reports on trans-Atlantic security, Europe, and Russia. Janusz is a regular speaker at the Post-Russia Forums, where the captive nations of the Russian Federation plan their futures after Russia's rupture.

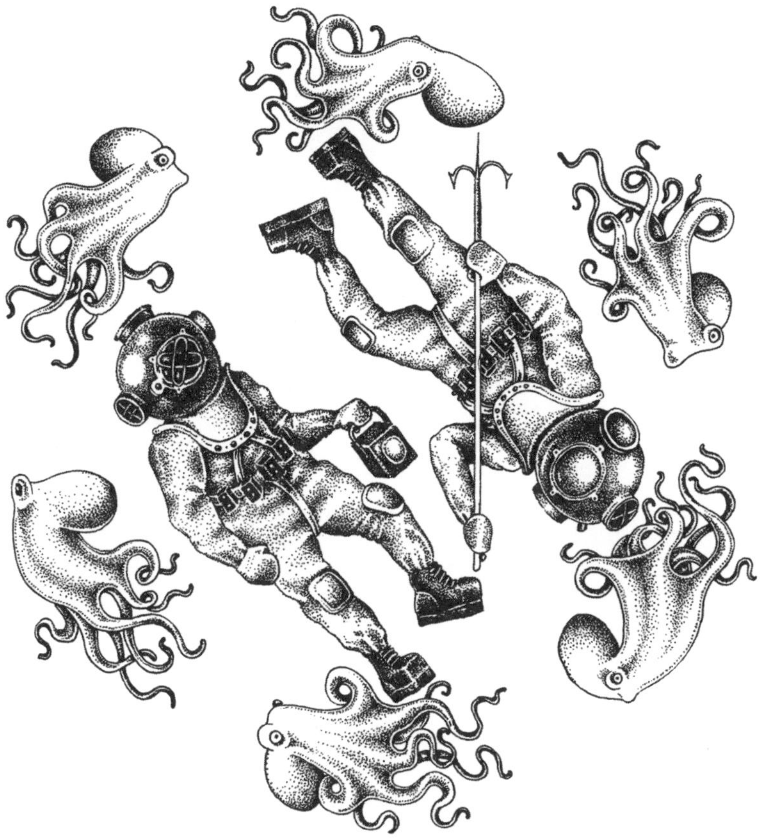

ILLUSTRATORS

Ivan Volianskyi
instagram.com/_dirtyneedles

Kateryna Sova
instagram.com/ket_eule

Iryna Lysenko
instagram.com/lysenko_ira
behance.net/IraLysenko

Maryna Lutsyk
instagram.com/maryna_lutsyk

Oleh Smal
facebook.com/olegsmalart

Andrii Yermolenko
instagram.com/andriy_yermolenko
facebook.com/AndriyYermolenkoArt

Olenka Zahorodnyk
instagram.com/alekon_zahorodnyk
behance.net/olenkazaho9602

Mykhailo Aleksandrov
behance.net/mishaaleks

Oleksandr Terez
instagram.com/alex.terez
behance.net/alexterez

Julia Maystruk
dribbble.com/jumaystrukart
instagram.com/ju_maystruk_art